deadly intentions

ANASTASI FAMILY SYNDICATE
BOOK 4

DORI PULITANO

BEHIND THE BADGE PRESS

family tree

Giuseppe Anastasi & Vittoria Anastasi
Grandfather/Deceased & Grandmother/live in Sicily

Giacomo Anastasi
Son to Giuseppe & Vittoria
Mafia Head in Sicily

Giorga Anastasi
Giacomo's Wife

Massimo Anastasi
Oldest son to Giacomo/Giorga/Mafia Head in Vegas/Owns
Discoteca Club

Madison Heart
Massimo's Fiancée

Vincenzo Anastasi
Second in Line/son to Giacomo/Giorga/Owns Bellissimo
Amore Restaurant

Riley Lawson
Vincenzo's Wife/Former FBI

Robert Deminico Anastasi & Veronica Gia Anastasi
Vincenzo & Riley's Twins

Antonio Anastasi
Third in Line/Son to Giacomo/Giorga/Owns Anastasi
Construction

Rachel Hill
Wife to Antonio &
Michael/Former Assistant
DA

Michael Brighton
Husband to Rachel &
Antonio/Anastasi Family
Attorney

Catarina Anastasi
Daughter to Giacomo/Giorga/Nurse

Donny Russo
Husband to Catarina/Massimo's Head Enforcer

Celestina Anastasi
21 years old
College Student
10-1-2002

Carmela Anastasi
21 years old
College Student
10-1-2002

notable characters

Alex Coulter
Former Detective/Head of Security at Discoteca (Massimo's Club)

Mike Donovan
District Attorney

Drew Mancini
Enforcer/Harley's Husband

Kevin Luchasi
Anastasi Family Doctor

Manuel Costa
Javier's Brother/New Gang Leader

Cristian Silva
Chilean Mafia/Matias Brother/Alliance with Anastasis

Filippo Bianchi
Don to Italian Mafia (Rome)/Alliance with Anastasis

Carlisle Casteneli
Former Detective/Head of Security at Discoteca (Massimo's Club)

Harley Cook
Catarina's Friend/Nurse/Drew's Wife

Miguel Angel
Sureños Leader/Alliance with Anastasi Family

Javier Costa
Gang Leader/Deceased

Matias Silva
Head of Chilean Mafia/Alliance with Anastasis

Bastian Silva
Chilean Mafia/ Matias Brother /Alliance with Anastasis

Lorenzo Bianchi
Son to Italian Mafia Don (Rome)/Alliance with Anastasis

series reading order

DANGEROUS ATTRACTION

MASSIMO & MADISON'S BOOK

DARK DESIRE

VINCENZO & RILEY'S BOOK

FATAL LOVE

ANTONIO, MIA & MICHAEL'S BOOK

DEADLY INTENTIONS

CATARINA & DONNY'S BOOK

CARNAGE HEART (NOVELLA)

BECKETT'S STORY

SAVAGE HEARTS

CELESTINA & BECKETT'S STORY

FRACTURED DEVOTION

CARMELLA & ALEX'S BOOK

Grab the entire series on E-Book at
https://alphabookboyfriends.com/collections/bundles/bundles

reader warning

Like most Mafia books, this one contains scenes that may be difficult for some to handle. Human trafficking, violence, and attempted suicide are all addressed in this book. If that is not something you can handle, please discontinue reading.

Suicide is a serious matter. If you or anyone you know in the United States is contemplating suicide, please seek help by reaching out to the Suicide & Crisis lifeline by dialing 988 from your phone. International assistance is available by clicking here.

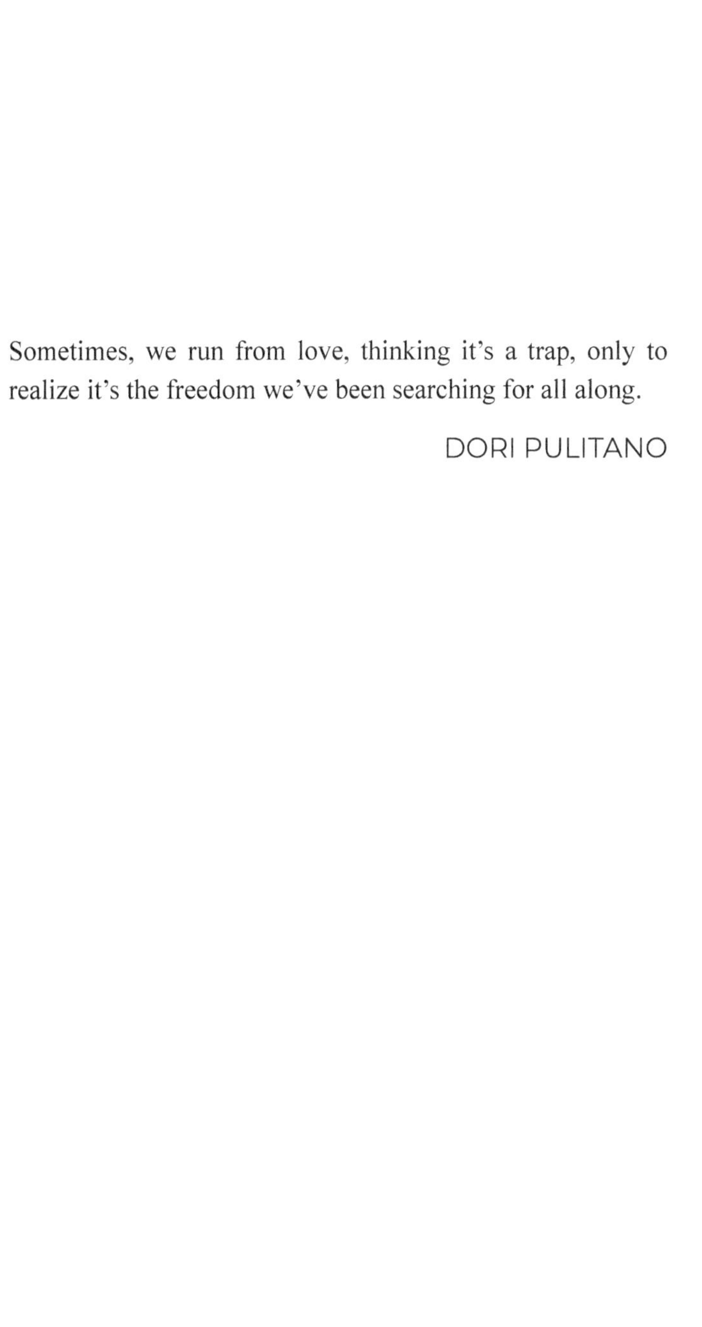

Sometimes, we run from love, thinking it's a trap, only to realize it's the freedom we've been searching for all along.

DORI PULITANO

one

CATARINA

ONE MONTH—THAT'S how long I'd been in the tiny town of Lake District. Though I stuck out like a sore thumb, no one knew who I really was. The new name I'd given myself was my security blanket. It allowed me to pretend I finally escaped the suffocation of being an Anastasi. For years, I lived in the shadow of my brothers and the family name. Now, for the first time, I felt free—even if it was a delusion.

"Trina," Harley, the nursing supervisor, called out to me, her voice echoing through the sterile hallway. "Can you meet a detective in room 305? He needs to get some fingerprints again from your patient. The last set found nothing."

"Are they serious?" I muttered. The frustration was evident in my tone. "Didn't they notice his hands the last time they were in here?" I shook my head, feeling a pang of sympathy for the unconscious man.

I understood their need to identify our unknown victim, but patience seemed to be in short supply. The poor guy had been here just as long as I had and had yet to show any signs of waking up. Apparently, there had been no hits on the DNA they got when he first arrived, but that only meant he wasn't in the system as a criminal. Grabbing his chart, I headed down the hallway to his room.

When I stepped inside, my spine stiffened at the sight of the man leaning against the wall. He was not one of the officers I'd met in the short time I'd been here, which made me go on high alert.

"Can I help you?" I snapped, moving toward the patient's bedside, and dropping his chart on the table with a thud.

He stood to his full height, a good five inches above my own, and stepped forward. "Good morning," he said, extending his hand. "I'm Detective Coulter."

Reluctantly, I slid my palm into his. The electric current that passed between us made me jerk my hand back quicker than I meant to. He noticed my reaction and smirked.

"Trina Aniston. You're new." He shot me a grin that made my cheeks heat with embarrassment. "Sorry… what I meant to say is, how can I help you, detective?"

"Yes, I'm new to the department and have been assigned this case. I'm trying to figure out who this man is, and as you know…" He paused, his eyes flicking to the patient for a moment before coming back to me. "We still haven't been able to identify him. I'd like to try for a new set of prints."

"Since you're new, I'm going to assume you aren't aware of his injuries," I scoffed, folding my arms across my chest. "Let me bring you up to speed." I flicked open the file and started reading. "John Doe arrived in the ER barely alive. Both his wrists and his right shoulder were broken. He suffered a punctured lung, a ruptured spleen, and significant head trauma. But that isn't even the worst of it." I pointed to his still form on the bed. "His fingers were crushed on both hands, and if that wasn't enough, three of his fingers on his left hand are gone." I held the detective's gaze. To my surprise, he didn't flinch at my words.

I lifted my stethoscope and pressed the silver metal against John Doe's chest. This man had endured something horrific, and while I knew we needed to figure out who he was, I wasn't going to let them treat him like trash. Detective Coulter watched me as I changed out his fluids and reset the machine.

"Doesn't he deserve us figuring out who he is?" Coulter stepped closer to the bed and pointed to him. "What if he has a family looking for him?"

My mind immediately went to my brothers. I knew they were probably looking for me, even though I'd asked them not to. This man's family probably hadn't expected him to just disappear without a trace. Guilt wormed its way into my chest.

"Yes," I sighed. "But at what cost? Can't you wait until he wakes up? Every time we unwrap his hands, we risk infection. He's already lost a part of himself. Are you willing to risk him losing his entire hand?"

"No, I don't want to put him at risk." Coulter ran his hand down his face, a gesture of frustration. "Any idea when he'll wake up?"

"You know we can't predict that, but—" I checked him over and tugged the sheet around him. "He's scheduled for another MRI this afternoon. Perhaps we'll know more then. I can have the doctor call you."

"I'll be back tonight." He stepped around me and paused. His body was close to mine when he leaned in and spoke softly. "You can give me an update then."

"Right." I stepped away and turned. "Nice meeting you, Detective," I said through a clenched jaw.

"The pleasure was all mine, Trina." He held out a cardstock square. "My card...in case he wakes up before I get back."

Detective Coulter stepped out, leaving me alone with our unknown victim. I dragged a chair to his bedside and sat down, needing a minute to gather myself. Alex Coulter had rattled me—but not in the way I had been expecting. The shock I felt when we touched made my body pulse with desire, leaving me confused. For as long as I could remember, there had only been one man who made my blood burn with need. But that was in a past life—a life I desperately wanted to forget.

A man like Alex Coulter could complicate my life in ways I didn't need. No matter how sexy he was, he was a cop, and I wasn't the woman everyone believed I was.

"Who are you, John Doe?" I pressed my hand to his forearm and sighed. "Are you a victim of an accident, or were you running from something like me?" I stood and straightened my scrubs. "I'll help figure out who you are. I promise."

I might have willingly walked away from my life, but this man didn't choose to be alone in this place. I would make it my personal mission to figure out where he came from—he just needed to wake up first.

"Trina." Harley smiled at me from behind the desk, her eyes sparkling with curiosity. "Who was that hunk of a man? I've never seen him before."

"Alex Coulter—the *detective*.'" I made air quotes when I said the last part, rolling my eyes. "He's new and has been assigned the case for our John Doe."

"I'd like him to cuff me." Harley waggled her eyebrows mischievously.

I rolled my eyes, but not before she caught the blush that crept up my neck.

"Ooh… you think he's sexy, too," she teased, a knowing smirk on her face.

"Not interested," I retorted, tossing the patient's folder onto the table, and leaning my head onto the cool surface, hoping to hide my embarrassment.

"Why not? You're hot as hell, and he's…fuckable," Harley declared with a grin.

"Harley." I lifted my head and stared at her, trying to be serious.

"You've been here…what, a month?" She shook her head when I didn't respond, undeterred. "You need to get out and have some fun. In fact—" she pushed to a stand. Her enthusiasm was infectious. "A couple of us are going out this Saturday. You should come. Meet the gang and have some drinks. Maybe you'll get lucky and get laid."

"Jesus." I pushed off the counter and started toward the breakroom, feeling overwhelmed.

"Come on. Would it kill you to have some fun? I'm starting to wonder if your vagina is broken." Harley caught up to me, her smile unwavering.

"Fine. If I go out with you guys, will you stop talking about my vagina?" I asked, exasperated.

"Promise." She drew an X across her chest, sealing the deal.

"Great. I'm going to grab a bite to eat." I hurried into the staff lounge and grabbed my lunch from the fridge. After plopping my ass onto the sofa, I unwrapped my sandwich and took a bite.

The truth was, I hadn't been with anyone in a long time. I closed my eyes and conjured up a memory I'd buried deep.

"I can't get you out of my head. Can't you see I love you?" His voice was raw with emotion, his eyes pleading.

"You shouldn't love me. I don't want to be part of your world, and you can't walk away. My brother wouldn't let you." I stared into his eyes and blinked back the tears, my heart breaking.

"I'd give it all up if it meant I got to have you."

"You'd do that for me?" I palmed his cheek and sighed, the weight of our reality pressing down on me.

"I told you... I love you, kitten." He pressed his lips to mine, and for a moment, the world melted away.

"I'm sorry. I can't love you the way you need. But I can give you this—even if it's only for tonight."

My chest burned with regret. Walking away from the only man I'd ever loved was nearly impossible. He hadn't been lying when he said he'd give it all up to be with me, but I knew the promise of his words wasn't possible. The life my family lived was something you couldn't get out of—not without disappearing or dying, and neither of those was an option for him. That next morning, I waited for him to leave, and I ran.

I fingered the stiff paper in my pocket and blew out a frustrated breath as I pulled it out. Reading over Detective Coulter's name and number, I closed my eyes and fought the guilt churning in my gut. I wasn't looking for love—I'd found that already—but maybe he was just the distraction I needed. The longer my heart ached for a man I couldn't have, the harder it was going to be to stick with my intentions of achieving a new life.

I tucked Detective Coulter's card back into my pocket, determination settling in my chest. Whatever the future held, I would face it head-on. I had to—for myself, and for the man lying in the hospital bed, waiting for someone to uncover his identity.

As I stood up and headed back to my duties, a sense of resolve washed over me. It was time to stop running and start living, one step at a time.

two

CATARINA

I STARED at my reflection in the mirror and grimaced. Somehow, I was sticking to my promise to go out with Harley and some of the other nurses. As much as the thought terrified me, I knew wallowing around my house would lead to dumb decisions. I couldn't count how many times I'd picked up the phone and called him—just to hear his voice. I never spoke, only listened as he demanded to know who was on the other end. It was a dangerous game. I needed to find a distraction before I broke down and gave myself away.

With the black handbag tucked under my arm, I grabbed my keys and headed out. The bar was a five-minute walk from my house, so I opted to go on foot. It was a glorious thing being able to walk somewhere without the fear of being snatched up and tortured. After my close encounter with kidnapping months ago, I thought I'd never feel safe doing something like this.

The moment I stepped inside the bar, I spotted Harley. She was seated toward the back with a few people I recognized. When she saw me in the doorway, her hand shot up and waved me over. I tipped my head up in acknowledgment and motioned toward the bar.

I saddled up to the bar and slid onto a stool. The bartender nodded toward me, telling me he'd be there in a second. Glancing around, I took in the scene as I waited. The air was filled with laughter and the clinking of glasses, a comforting backdrop to my nerves.

I knew the minute Detective Coulter was behind me. My body tingled with awareness, and I sucked in a breath.

"Fancy seeing you here." His warm breath hissed across my neck, causing goosebumps to erupt across my skin.

"Detective," I said without turning around, my voice steadier than I felt.

"Not tonight. Tonight, I'm just Alex." He slid beside me and propped his elbow on the wooden surface. "You here alone?"

"No." I glanced toward the corner, only to see Harley give me two thumbs up. "I'm here with some coworkers." His eyes followed my line of sight.

"I see. Can I buy you a drink?"

I held his gaze for a moment. A distraction, my brain whispered.

"Sure. That'd be nice of you."

While I waited for him to place our order, I let my eyes dance over his body. Alex Coulter was definitely handsome. Harley had been right about that assessment. He was well over six feet tall, and in casual clothes, I could see a bit more of his build. His brown hair was cut short, giving me a perfect view of his chiseled jawline. He had beautiful blue eyes that twinkled when he spoke, drawing me in. Alex was extremely fit—the tightness of his shirt did little to hide the toned physique beneath the cotton material. I was so caught up in ogling his body, I didn't notice him watching me. I jumped when he cleared his throat. Pink tinged my cheeks as I forced my eyes up to find his gaze glimmering with laughter.

"Like what you see?"

I grabbed the drink in his hand and guzzled it down, feeling the burn of the alcohol mix with my embarrassment. Alex tipped his own glass to his lips and sipped the amber liquid, his eyes never leaving mine. He set the glass down and took the one I was hiding behind and placed it on the bar.

"I didn't mean to embarrass you." He brushed a loose lock from my face, his touch sending a shiver down my spine. "Tell me about yourself." He sat back and waited for me to answer, his gaze open and curious.

"Not much to tell, I'm afraid. I needed a change of scenery and found this job. And here I am." I smiled, trying to keep it light.

"Come on, there's got to be more to you than that," he coaxed, his eyes twinkling. "What made you leave your old life behind?"

I hesitated, the question hitting too close to home. "Sometimes you just need a fresh start, you know?"

He nodded. His expression was thoughtful. "I get that. Everyone's got something they're running from or running to."

"What about you?" I asked, turning the tables. "What's your story?"

Alex chuckled, taking another sip of his drink. "Not much to tell either. Just a guy who loves his job and the thrill of the chase. I'm originally from Montana. Former Army ranger. I was injured on deployment and decided it was time to get out."

I raised an eyebrow. "Wow, former military to cop. Detective work must be interesting."

"It has its moments," he agreed. "But enough about me. What do you do when you're not working?"

I laughed softly. "Honestly, not much. I'm still settling in, trying to get a feel for the place. But I like to read, go for walks, that sort of thing."

He leaned in closer, his eyes locking onto mine. "Maybe I could show you around sometime. Help you get to know the area better."

My heart skipped a beat at his suggestion. "Maybe," I said, trying to play it cool. "That could be nice."

"Great," he said, his smile widening. "How about this weekend?"

Before I could respond, Harley appeared beside us, a playful grin on her face. "I see you two are getting along just fine."

"Harley," I groaned, feeling my cheeks heat again. "We're just talking."

"Uh-huh," she said, clearly not convinced. "Well, don't let me interrupt. I just wanted to make sure you're having a good time."

"I am, thanks," I replied, giving her a grateful smile.

"Good. Now, if you'll excuse me, I have some dancing to do," she said with a wink, heading back to our table.

Alex watched her go, then turned back to me. "Your friend seems like a lot of fun."

"She is," I agreed. "A bit nosy, but her heart's in the right place."

He laughed. "Nosy friends are the best. They keep life interesting."

"True," I said, feeling more at ease. "So, this weekend, huh?"

"Yeah," he said, his expression hopeful. "I promise it'll be fun."

I took a deep breath, feeling a mix of excitement and apprehension. "Okay. This weekend it is."

"Perfect," he said, raising his glass. "To new beginnings."

"To new beginnings," I echoed, clinking my glass against his.

As the night wore on, I found myself opening up more, the walls I'd built around my heart slowly crumbling. Maybe Harley was right. Maybe a little fun and a little distraction were exactly what I needed. And maybe, just maybe, Alex Coulter was the perfect person to help me find it. He talked about his decision to leave his team in the military and put down roots.

"And you chose here?" I asked, curious.

"Yep. A buddy of mine grew up here and talked about the serenity of the place. After all the turmoil I've lived with, serene sounded nice."

I sipped the remnants of my drink and smiled. Alex noticed my glass was empty and grinned.

"You want another?"

"Sure. Tonight's about letting loose."

"Is it now?" He grinned as the bartender set a fresh drink down.

Harley approached us with a shit-eating grin and thrust her hand out.

"Hello, Detective. We haven't met yet. I'm Harley Cook, the nursing supervisor at the hospital."

"Nice to meet you, Harley. Alex Coulter. I'm a new detective with the P.D."

"Right. Anyway, sorry to interrupt, but a few of us are heading out to the ski lodge. They've got some live music, and we want to dance. You going to come?" She turned toward me and grinned. "Or are you gonna finally get that thing fixed?"

My eyes widened with embarrassment, but fortunately Alex didn't know what she was talking about.

"Maybe I can help you fix it." He glanced between us, confusion marring his expression.

"Oh, I think you most definitely could," Harley said.

I slapped her arm playfully, causing her to roar with laughter.

"I feel like I'm missing something here." Alex scratched his head as he glanced between us.

"You go on ahead. I might catch up later." I shook my head as she waved goodbye. Turning back to Alex, I smiled apologetically. "Sorry about her. She can be a lot."

"It's all good, but what was she talking about?" Alex flicked his eyes to the door briefly before taking a sip of his drink.

"She's worried about my ability to get laid."

Alex choked on his drink, spewing the dark liquid across my chest. "Fuck." He grabbed a few napkins and started dabbing the wet droplets on my skin.

I sucked in a breath when he patted the tissue down my breast and paused. "I'm good." I grabbed his hand and lifted it from my chest.

"Christ. I wasn't expecting that. I'm—"

Leaning across his stool, I pressed my lips to his. I barely knew the man, but as Harley said, I needed to loosen up. Alex stiffened beneath me for a moment before relenting and giving in to the kiss.

His mouth parted and his tongue swiped against mine. He dropped the napkins and wrapped his arms around my back, tugging my body into his. He tasted like whiskey and mint as my lips moved against his. When I finally broke the kiss, he blinked as if in a state of shock.

"That was a surprising turn of events." He sucked his bottom lip into his mouth.

"Sorry, I shouldn't have done that." I closed my eyes in embarrassment.

"Why not? I wanted to kiss you the first time I met you in John Doe's hospital room."

"You did?" My eyes shot open in surprise.

"Yes." His thumb swiped across my bottom lip. "You're a gorgeous woman, Trina."

My mind stilled as my own words rattled inside—a distraction.

"You want to get out of here?" I stood and grabbed my clutch. "I have something that needs fixing at my house, and I can't do it alone." I started toward the door.

"Sure. I guess." Alex stood and threw some money on the bar.

"I just live a few minutes this way. Hope you don't mind walking."

"Not at all, but what exactly am I fixing?" He asked, curiosity mingling with amusement in his voice.

I gave him a seductive grin over my shoulder as we stepped out the door onto the sidewalk.

"My vagina."

three

HOLY SHIT. I couldn't believe I'd just said that to him. I fully expected him to turn around and hightail it to his car, but he didn't. In fact, he hadn't said a damn word since I spoke the words out loud. We got to my house, and he followed me up the steps to the door.

"Now's your chance to leave." I slipped the key in without looking back at him.

As soon as I got the door open, Alex's hands gripped my waist and spun me to face him. He shoved me inside and kicked the door closed with his foot as his mouth fastened over mine. It was like a switch had been flipped, and I was desperate for a man's touch. I clawed at his shirt, silently begging him to take it off. When he obliged, I groaned in satisfaction. Just as I had expected, his body was a work of art.

His palms gripped my ass, lifting me off the floor. My legs instinctively wrapped around his waist as he pressed me into the wall, his erection digging into the apex of my thighs. Pinning my arms to the wall, he licked his way down the side of my neck. Alex sucked and nibbled the tender flesh, making me moan loudly.

"Fuck, you're driving me wild with those noises," he whispered against my throat.

He set me down and fingered the dress I wore. Dropping to his knees, Alex bunched the material around my waist and ripped my thong off. He shoved a finger between my legs, the roughness of it making my body clench around his digit.

"I'm not a gentle lover, Trina. If you want me to stop, you need to tell me." He pumped his finger in and out of my core.

"I'm not looking for gentle." I spread my legs, giving him better access. "Do your best."

Alex blinked for a moment, then dove face first into my pussy. His tongue lashed out, swirling around my swollen nub as he thrust his fingers in hard. The orgasm was sudden, nearly knocking me off my feet, but Alex used his shoulder to pin me in place. He lapped up my release, never relenting in his touch. I tugged at his hair, urging him to stand.

"Bedroom," I whimpered into the cool air.

Alex took the cue and scooped me up. I wrapped my legs around him again, my dripping wet center pressed against the bulge in his pants. Somehow, he found my room and tossed me onto the bed.

"Fuck," he grunted as he climbed onto the bed above me.

His fingers trailed sparks of electricity down my side as he moved his palm between my legs. He flicked the swollen nub, causing me to tense with the sensation of my impending orgasm. Through hooded eyelids, I watched as he pushed his pants down and sheathed himself in a condom. He moved between my legs and paused.

"Last chance to change your mind." He bit his lip, giving me an out.

A moment of panic struck me hard, and I blinked. What was I doing? I barely knew this man, and I'd brought him home. Alex must have seen the indecision in my eyes because he rolled off me and propped himself on his side.

"You okay?" He pressed his hand to my shoulder.

"Yeah." I forced the lie out. "I'm sorry I ruined the moment. It's just…" I licked my lips and sighed. "You're the first man I've done this with, and I kind of freaked out."

"Wait… you're a virgin?" Alex's eyes widened as he held my gaze.

"I mean, I've never brought a man home for a fling like this. I've only been with one other guy, and the breakup wasn't easy. I'm sorry about this." I covered my face with my arm and turned away from him in embarrassment.

"Hey." Alex tugged my elbow, uncovering my eyes. "Don't. I'm not mad. I want you, Trina. I won't lie about that. But if you're not ready, then I'll wait. I didn't want this to be a one-night stand, anyway."

"Really?" I blinked back the shame of my actions.

"Yes. If you'll excuse me, I need to borrow your bathroom and take care of this." He waved his hand down toward his erect penis still covered in the barrier. "If you don't mind, I'm going to hop in the shower—a cold one."

"Sure." I nodded. "Of course."

As soon as the door closed, I sat up and pulled the sheet around my body. Listening as the shower kicked on, I grimaced. I was acting like a child, but for some reason, the thought of sleeping with him made my heart race. I wiped away the wetness gathering in my eyes, unwilling to let my emotions get the better of me. Alex stepped out and froze. He held my gaze in his and narrowed his eyes.

"You sure you're okay?"

"I think you should go." The words were out before I could stop them. On the verge of a meltdown, I blinked, fighting back the tears.

The last thing I needed was for him to feel bad about what happened. It wasn't as though I hadn't enjoyed it—I had—but he was a fucking cop, and I couldn't let him get close. This couldn't go anywhere, and I knew it. I also knew the reason for my panic was the one thing I couldn't have—and that made it worse.

"Did I do something wrong?"

"No." I shook my head.

"Because if I pressured you, I'm sorry. I didn't expect this, but it doesn't change the fact that I enjoyed tonight… a lot." He sat down on the bed and pressed his hand to my knee. "Talk to me, Trina."

"It's fine. Really. I didn't do anything I didn't want to, but this—" I waved between us and sighed. "Can't happen."

"Why not? Are you married or something?"

I laughed. "Definitely not, but I moved here for a fresh start, and a relationship isn't something I want right now."

"I see." He stood and grabbed his pants. "I like you, but I get it. It doesn't change the fact I'd like to get to know you, Trina."

"You would?" I blinked.

"Yes. Maybe we could go on an actual date."

"I told you I don't want a relationship. I can't."

"I don't understand." He slipped his shirt on and shoved his feet into his shoes.

"Please, just go, Alex. This was a mistake. I'm sorry if I led you on. And I swear, this isn't something I normally do. I need some time to figure things out. I'm not looking for a relationship, but I wasn't expecting this attraction."

"Then let me take you on a proper date. Start over."

"I don't know." I bit my lip, torn.

"Just one date. It's not complicated, Trina."

"That's the thing… you don't know me," I sighed.

"All the more reason to go on a date with me."

I knew I was taking a risk, but the thought of being alone terrified me more.

"One date."

Alex leaned forward and pressed a chaste kiss to my lips. "I'm going before you change your mind." He started out my bedroom door. "I'll see you this week at the hospital. Be thinking about where you want to go." Without another word, he was gone.

I flopped back on the bed and groaned. What had I done? I was supposed to be lying low until I got established. A relationship with anyone would put me at risk for exposing who I really was, and I was going on a date—with a freaking cop.

I rolled over and screamed into my pillow. Life was supposed to be easier here—a new name, a new me—and here I'd gone and slept with a detective. My mind shot to my brothers. It must have been in our blood to attract cops because Vincenzo's wife was former law enforcement. I clenched my eyes closed. Thinking about my brother conjured up the vision of him, which led to more guilt. I'd only slept with one man in my life, and he didn't know that he'd been my first.

A tear slipped down my cheek and splashed onto the pillow. How was I going to move on when I couldn't even have sex with another man without thinking about him? I screamed out again, hurling the pillow across the room.

So much for a distraction. All I got instead was a complication I wasn't prepared for.

What else could go wrong?

CATARINA

WELL?" Harley cocked her hip and stood, blocking my path, her expression demanding an explanation.

"Well, what?" I tried to step around her, but she grabbed my arm. Her grip was firm and unyielding.

"Nope, you're not getting off that easy. What happened with the hot cop?"

"I freaked out and kicked him out of my house," I admitted, my voice barely above a whisper.

"You… wait, come again?" Harley shook her head in disbelief. "It sounded like you said you kicked him out of your house."

"I did. I couldn't bring myself to have sex with him."

Harley's mouth popped open. Her eyes were wide with shock. She closed her mouth suddenly and narrowed her eyes, scrutinizing me.

"What did he do?" she asked, her voice filled with concern.

"He understood and asked to take me on a date," I replied, shrugging my shoulders as if it was no big deal.

"He likes you," Harley smirked, leaning in closer. "He does. No man would ask you on a date after being kicked out before sex. Sounds like the detective wants something more than a fling."

"I can't date him," I said, blowing out a frustrated breath, feeling the weight of my past and my secrets pressing down on me.

"Why not? You're a single girl, he's a single guy, right?" Harley persisted. Her tone was gentle yet firm.

"Yes, but my life is complicated, and I came here to start over without added complications. My intentions were to establish myself, then worry about dating."

"Sometimes, the best outcomes aren't what you plan," Harley said, patting my back and giving me a sympathetic smile. "Why not see where it goes? You don't have to keep dating if it causes too much stress. But not giving him a chance may cause you to kick yourself later on."

"You're right," I sighed, feeling the tension ease a bit. "I need to give the man a chance—as long as he doesn't figure out my secret, it could work. I have to go check on John Doe. Talk later?"

"Yep. Holler if you need anything." Harley disappeared around the corner, leaving me to stare at the empty hallway.

The beeping of the machines filled the tiny room as I shut myself inside. I checked his vitals and adjusted his fluids before pulling up a chair and sitting down. The nightshift nurse had bathed him and changed his dressing before I'd arrived. His most recent test results showed brain activity that appeared to be normal, but until he woke up, we wouldn't know the extent of his damage. I ran my palm down his arm and sighed.

"Hey there, bud. I wish we knew who you were. I hate calling you John Doe." I tugged the sheet tighter and tucked it under his arm.

"In fact, I think I'll call you Johnny. Makes it more personal." I felt foolish talking to an unconscious man, but something about him made me feel safe. Maybe because I knew he wouldn't talk back.

"So… I agreed to a date with the cop trying to figure out who you are. Am I stupid for saying yes? Hell, I almost slept with him, Johnny, but I couldn't go through with it. I've only ever slept with one man, and he's ruined me, I think. I miss him. Was I smart running away like I did? I just couldn't live that life anymore, but why does it hurt so much? I would've thought I'd be over him by now. Stupid, right?"

"What's stupid?" Alex's deep timber voice caused me to jump. "Sorry. Didn't mean to startle you."

I pushed back and stood, my heart racing. "What are you doing here?" I moved the chair back to the corner and straightened my shirt, trying to compose myself.

"I wanted to see if there had been any change in his condition." Alex glanced toward John Doe.

"Johnny is still the same," I said, avoiding his gaze.

"Johnny?" Alex furrowed his brows. "You gave him a nickname?"

"Yep. John Doe seems so impersonal, and I spend a lot of time with him." I started toward the door, but he reached out and grabbed my arm.

"You haven't changed your mind about our date, have you?"

I glanced at the spot where his hand pressed against my skin. Alex was a good-looking man, but I didn't get the same spark from him I'd felt from someone else. But this was my chance to reinvent myself.

"No, I haven't." I forced a smile, still unsure if my decision had been the right one.

Alex tugged me to stand in front of him and brushed my hair from my face, his touch gentle yet firm.

"I can see you fighting yourself on this. What are you afraid of?"

The air whooshed from my lungs, and I stilled, unable to meet his gaze.

"I don't trust myself, Alex. I gave my heart to someone else, and it didn't work out. I came here for a fresh start and wasn't planning on this." I waved my hand between us. "I just need some time to…"

"To get over your heartbreak." Alex stepped back, his expression softening. "Then we can start out as friends, and if something more comes of it, I'd be thrilled. But Trina—" he shoved his hands into his pockets. "You deserve to be happy, whatever that looks like. Now…" He gripped the doorknob. "I'll be at your house Saturday at six."

"Okay." My voice came out in a whisper, the weight of his words settling over me.

Alex leaned in and pressed a kiss to my forehead, his lips warm and reassuring.

"See you later," he said softly.

The door closed behind him, and I blew out the breath I'd been holding. This was when I needed my family. Whenever I was confused, I sought their advice. But now, I couldn't do that.

Looking at Johnny's broken body made me think of the life I'd run away from. The people I loved were dealing with so much, and I probably only added to their stress. The day I left Vegas, I knew it would create a ripple effect of pain I likely could never take back.

They were still reeling from the loss of Antonio and Mia's partner, Michael. The day I'd met Mia, I learned he was in love with two people. It was weird, but seeing the love Michael and Mia had for my brother told me all I needed to know. Then Michael had been taken. Just more of my family's shitty business dealings ruining the lives of people it touched.

Even as I sat there and wondered about the unknown man lying in front of me, I wondered if his life had been as complicated as mine. There had been speculation that John Doe had been involved with a local gang—even this small town had criminal issues to deal with. Seeing him bandaged up and broken, I wondered if he was just in the wrong place at the wrong time— like I had been so many times. I smoothed down the blanket covering his still-black-and-blue body and sighed. It didn't matter the reason. No one deserved to be diminished to a shell of a human.

"Johnny, I think I've made more of a mess of my life than I wanted. All I wanted was my own life, my own dreams. Coming here was supposed to be easy, but like they say… the road to hell is paved with good intentions."

My words echoed in the silent room, and I felt a wave of sadness wash over me. I had come here to escape, to start fresh, but it seemed like my past was always just a step behind me. I glanced at Johnny's still form, my heart heavy with the weight of my choices.

"What do you think, Johnny?" I whispered, my voice trembling. "Do you think I can really start over? Or am I just fooling myself?"

The steady beeping of the machines was my only answer, a reminder of the fragility of life and the uncertainty of the future. I reached out and gently squeezed Johnny's hand, feeling a connection to this stranger that I couldn't quite explain.

"I'll figure it out," I promised, more to myself than to him. "Somehow, I'll figure it out."

As I sat there, watching over Johnny, I felt a glimmer of hope. Maybe, just maybe, things could work out. Maybe I could find a way to balance my past with my future. And maybe, Alex was right—I deserved to be happy, whatever that looked like.

CATARINA

THIS DAY COULDN'T DRAG on any longer than it had. My mind wouldn't shut off last night after I got home. All I could think about was Johnny lying in that bed alone and how I left the people who loved me without a care for their feelings. When I came to this tiny town, I hadn't expected the guilt of my actions to weigh so heavily on me. And now, walking through the narrow corridor of the hospital, all I could think about was the loneliness I'd subjected myself to.

John Doe—or Johnny, as I'd grown accustomed to calling him—was improving each day. He still hadn't regained consciousness, but his injuries were beginning to heal nicely. In fact, there was a possibility all the bandages would come off soon. I wondered what he would look like. Would we finally be able to identify him and give his family some kind of peace?

Needing to clarify the newest orders for his treatment, I made my way toward Doctor Brooks's office. Doctor Brooks was not the most personable man to deal with, but he knew his shit. He'd recently changed around some of Johnny's meds, making me concerned about the long-term effects the increase might have on him. It wasn't uncommon for nurses to ask for clarification of protocols when dealing with patients, but Brooks wasn't particularly fond of anyone questioning his decisions, which is why Harley sent me on this mission. She hated him—like hated with a passion, hated. I assumed there was more to the story, but I never pressed. We all had our secrets.

The door to his office was cracked slightly, giving me a partial view of him inside. I knocked but paused when I realized he wasn't alone. Another man stood in front of his desk, and it appeared that they were having a heated discussion. Their voices, while slightly muffled, filtered through the opening.

"I told you. It's taken care of." Doctor Brooks shifted on his feet behind the desk.

"I don't need any more fuckups, Brooks. If this shipment doesn't come through, you'll pay. I won't be as kind as I was with the last fuck up you made."

I leaned toward the room, trying to hear more. As I stepped closer, the door shifted and groaned as it swung open. Both men froze, their gazes pinning me with an intense glare that made my blood coil with unease. It was a look I'd seen so many times with my brothers. Whatever I'd just walked in on wasn't something I was supposed to hear.

My throat constricted as I swallowed the bile. I left Vegas to avoid this feeling. Now, standing here in the tiny town of Lake District, I wondered what I'd stumbled into.

"Um… Doctor Brooks." I ran my palms down my scrubs and shifted my eyes between the two men. "I didn't mean to interrupt. I can come back later." I turned to make my escape but was halted by his voice.

"Wait," Brooks called, his tone brusque. "What do you need, Nurse Aniston?"

I forced a smile as I stood at the threshold of his office, feeling the weight of the other man's gaze burning into my side. "I just needed to clarify the new medication orders for John Doe in room 305. The increased dosage—"

"Is necessary," Brooks interrupted, his eyes narrowing. "You're not questioning my judgment, are you?"

"No, of course not," I stammered, my heart pounding in my chest. "I just wanted to ensure I understood the reasoning behind it, given his current condition."

I took a deep breath. "Ok, I just wanted to check." I glanced toward the man who was watching me with daggers in his eyes. "Sorry to have interrupted your meeting."

"Who is this lovely lady, Brooks?" the creepy guy asked as he stepped toward me.

Now that he was closer, I was able to get a better look at him. He was Hispanic, over six feet in height, with dark eyes. His penetrating gaze seemed to be trying to see into my soul as he lingered on my face. I blinked, trying to break the eerie trance he had me under, and stepped back.

"This is one of our newest nurses, Trina Aniston," Doctor Brooks grunted.

"Miss Aniston." He stepped close and took my hand in his. "I'm Javier Costa. It's very nice to meet you." Something familiar about his name tingled in the depths of my memory, but I pushed them down and forced a smile. "Tell me. Where does a beautiful nurse like you come from?"

"East." I tugged my hand away from his and turned toward Doctor Brooks. "I'll just come back later. I need to finish my rounds."

"I'm sure we'll see each other again," Javier sneered as I hurried from the room.

I pressed my back against the wall outside and blew out a breath. Whatever I'd walked in on had been something they didn't want me to hear. That was apparent in their body language. As I leaned there, wondering what in the hell just happened, I heard Javier's voice.

"Do you think she heard anything?"

"No, I don't think so," Brooks replied. "Even if she heard the tail end, she doesn't know what we were talking about."

"I hope so. The last thing you need is a loose end, Brooks. I'd hate to short you a nurse, especially a pretty one like that. You know I can't have loose lips."

I sucked in a breath and pushed off the wall. Moving as fast as I could, I ran down the hallway and locked myself inside the on-call room. What the fuck was Doctor Brooks involved in? Javier Costa didn't look like a businessman, at least, not one that would deal with the hospital. After calming down, I let myself out of the confines of the tiny enclosure and sought Harley. I was relieved to find her seated behind the main station on our floor.

"Trina." Harley looked up from the computer and grinned. "You ready for that hot date with the sexy detective?"

Just like that, she'd taken my mind off the weird encounter with Dr. Brooks. Thoughts of my date with Alex caused me to blush.

"I guess." I grinned, not knowing what more to say. I was still conflicted about saying yes to going out with him.

"You guess?" Harley cocked her eyebrow at me. "That man is hot, Trina. I'm not saying you have to marry him, but a nice roll in the hay would do you some good."

I snorted at her blatant comment. "Jesus."

"What?" Harley stood and leaned across the desk, her eyes twinkling mischievously. "I won't pretend to know what brought you here. You've been pretty tight-lipped. I'm going to go out on a limb and say it had something to do with a man. And if I'm right—" her voice dropped to a whisper. "A brand-new dick will help you move on."

"Wow." I blinked, a mix of amusement and embarrassment flooding my face. "You have no filter, Harley."

"I know. It's a gift. Now, let's grab some lunch and talk about what you're wearing."

"Right. Lunch." I followed her to the elevator and climbed in behind her, my thoughts still spinning from our conversation.

Just as the doors were closing, a hand halted them to a stop. My lungs stilled as Javier stepped inside and grinned.

"Miss Aniston. Pleasure running into you again." His voice rolled through the tiny box like nails on a chalkboard. "Who is your friend?"

Harley giggled, not realizing this man wasn't someone she should entertain. "I'm Harley Cook, the charge nurse in the ICU. And you are?"

"Javier Costa." He tugged her hand into his, pressed his lips to her knuckles, and grinned.

"Were you visiting someone in the ICU?" Harley tilted her head in question.

"No. I'm a business associate of Doctor Brooks. We were discussing some personal matters."

"Oh." Harley looked back at me and furrowed her brow. "Does that mean you're a doctor?"

His laugh made my skin crawl. "Heavens, no."

The doors dinged, signaling our arrival. Javier stepped out and waited for us to follow. He paused, turning to face us.

"Miss Aniston, I hope we meet again. You too, Miss Cook. Have a good day."

I watched as he walked toward the main entrance, my stomach churning with unease.

"That's one hell of a sexy dude. What are you? Some kind of sexy man magnet?" Harley joked. "Ever since you started working here, hot guys keep popping up."

"Hot doesn't always mean safe, Harley." I started toward the café, my mind racing. "Come on, let's go eat."

We found a quiet corner in the hospital café and settled into our seats. The moment I sat down, Harley's eyes sparkled with curiosity.

"So, spill. What's the plan for tonight? Where's he taking you?"

I shrugged, trying to sound casual. "He said he'd pick me up at six. I guess we'll figure it out from there."

Harley leaned forward. Her excitement was palpable. "You know, it's been a while since you had some fun. Maybe tonight is the start of something new."

"I hope so," I admitted, my voice soft. "But I can't shake this feeling that I'm getting myself into something complicated."

"Life's always complicated," Harley said, waving her hand dismissively. "But you can't let that stop you from living. Besides, you deserve to have a little happiness."

Her words resonated with me, and I found myself nodding. "You're right. I need to give this a chance."

"Atta girl," Harley cheered, raising her soda in a mock toast. "Now, let's talk outfits. You need to knock his socks off."

I laughed, feeling lighter for the first time in days. "All right, fashion guru. What do you suggest?"

Harley's eyes lit up as she launched into a detailed description of the perfect date outfit, her enthusiasm infectious. For a moment, I let myself get caught up in the excitement, pushing aside the unease that had settled in my stomach.

After lunch, we headed back to our floor, and I made my way to Johnny's room. As I entered, the familiar beeping of the machines greeted me, and I felt a sense of calm washing over me. Checking his vitals and adjusting his fluids, I sat down beside his bed.

"Hey, Johnny," I whispered, feeling the need to talk to him. "I've got a date tonight. Can you believe it? After everything, I'm finally trying to move on."

I glanced at his still form, wondering if he could somehow hear me. "Life's been a rollercoaster, hasn't it? But I'm trying to take control, trying to find some happiness."

The silence in the room was comforting, and I continued, "I know you're fighting your own battle. I promise I'll do everything I can to help you. And maybe, just maybe, we'll both find some peace."

The day flew by, and before I knew it, it was time to head home and get ready for my date. As I stood in front of my closet, Harley's fashion advice played in my head. I finally settled on a dress that was simple yet elegant, hoping it would make a good impression.

34

CATARINA

BY THE TIME Alex knocked on my door, my nerves were in overdrive. I took a deep breath and opened it, my heart skipping a beat at the sight of him. He looked effortlessly handsome, his eyes lighting up when he saw me.

Wow," he said, his voice filled with genuine admiration. "You look stunning, Trina."

"Thank you," I replied, feeling a blush creep up my cheeks. "You don't look so bad yourself."

He grinned and offered his arm. "Shall we?"

As we walked to his car, I felt a mix of excitement and apprehension. This was a new beginning, a chance to find some happiness. But the shadows of my past still lingered, a reminder of the secrets I carried.

We drove in comfortable silence, the city lights blurring past us. When we arrived at our destination, I was pleasantly surprised to see a charming little restaurant, its warm lights inviting. Lake City was popular for snow enthusiasts, making the resort a go-to destination. As we pulled down the long drive leading to the massive building, my breath hitched. It was beautiful.

The trees were changing colors for the impending winter, making the path to the lodge one out of story books. The lodge itself was something I would have expected to see in Italy, with its massive pillars and ornate design. It was unlike anything we had back in Vegas.

Alex pulled to the front and hopped out. The dress I was wearing clung to me as I slipped out of Alex's truck when the valet opened my door. He ushered me out just as Alex rounded the front of the truck. His palm pressed against the small of my back as he guided me to the entrance.

"Wow." My breath caught again as we stepped inside.

The foyer was just as stunning as the exterior. Massive chandeliers lit the hall with a soft yellow glow. Soft music wafted from the dining room off to the side, giving a romantic atmosphere to the lodge.

"You like it?" Alex smiled as we walked to the hostess.

"It's gorgeous." I shook my head, still in awe. "You didn't have to do all this, Alex. This is…" My voice trailed off as a woman greeted him.

"Follow me." She grinned, leading us to our table.

And fuck. The table she seated us at had a view I would remember for years to come. The sun was setting beyond the peaks of the mountain in the distance, bathing the valley in a beautiful pink hue.

"So," Alex said, and my attention snapped away from admiring the view. "Tell me about yourself, Trina."

I swallowed. This was the part I dreaded. I couldn't tell Alex about the real me, meaning this relationship was being built on a lie. A lie I could never come back from if he ever found out. I cleared my throat. The words were burning even before they were out.

"What would you like to know?" I sipped a glass of wine that had magically appeared in front of me.

"Whatever you're willing to share." He grinned as his lips wrapped around the glass he was holding.

"I have a big family, three brothers and two sisters." I kept it as close to the truth as possible to avoid any slips. I could share my story without sharing too much. Plus, talking about them made me feel close to them, even though I couldn't be.

Alex's eyebrows raised to his hairline in surprise. "Wow... six kids?"

"Yeah. It was pretty noisy growing up. I'm the oldest girl. I have two older brothers and one younger, then the twins, my sisters." I smiled, thinking about my sisters, Carmela, and Celestina. They were still in Italy finishing school but would eventually come to the States. At least, that had been their plan. I thought I'd be there when they finally settled in Vegas, but now... My heart stuttered with the realization I wouldn't be there. The pain was crushing, sending a pang of regret through my veins.

"Do you still speak to them? Your siblings?"

"Not as much as I should." The lie tasted bitter in my mouth. "My parents moved abroad, so I don't hear from them much now that I moved out here." Another lie. "What about you? Do you have any siblings?"

"No, only child. My mom passed away when I was seventeen from cancer, and my dad, well…he didn't take too highly to my career path. He wanted me to be a dentist, like him."

"A dentist? Really?" I sipped my drink, trying to imagine Alex in a white coat. "I definitely don't see that for you. Did you move here from Montana? I know you're new to the department."

"No, Reno. When I left the military, I was offered a job there and took it." He grinned, but my heart stopped.

"Reno?"

"Yeah. You ever been?"

"No, can't say that I have. I grew up in the east. Oregon is the first place in the west I've been."

"Really? Where in the east did you say you were from?"

"Um." I was about to speak, but the waiter saved me.

"Would you like to order?" He smiled at Alex and me, waiting for one of us to answer.

Alex placed our orders, his question forgotten for the time being. I wasn't sure how much longer I could keep up the charade, so I was thankful for the interruption. By the time the food had arrived, I learned Alex was working as part of a special task force. He was on loan from the Reno Police Department as part of an ongoing investigation that led them here. He was assigned to John Doe's case because they believed he was involved in the criminal investigation out of Reno.

"Isn't that Dr. Brooks?" Alex's question broke into my thoughts, and I followed his line of sight.

Sure enough, Dr. Brooks was seated toward the back of the restaurant, chatting up the same man from earlier—Javier Costa. I couldn't take my eyes off the two men. How could it be that they would wind up at the same location? This couldn't have been a coincidence. I'd seen it too many times at home with my brothers. Things like this didn't happen by chance. No. Those two men were here to send me a message—a message I was getting loud and clear.

"Yes, that's him. Weird seeing him here of all places." I forced a smile. My glass felt cool against my lips as I sipped my wine.

"He doesn't choose the best company," Alex grumbled.

"Why do you say that?"

"Javier Costa isn't a good guy." He sipped his drink, "I'd love to put him behind bars."

I swallowed hard, nearly choking on the liquid. Alex stood from his chair and moved beside me to pat my back. The commotion drew the attention of both men. Javier cut me a glance that made my blood run cold. My eyes never left his through my coughing fit. I watched as he withdrew his phone and talked into it. Dr. Brooks said something to him, his body language tense as he and Javier seemed to argue about something.

"Shit. You okay?"

"Yes." My cheeks burned with embarrassment as I nodded at his concern. "Went down the wrong pipe."

"How about we get out of here?" Alex flagged the waiter over and settled our bill.

"Perfect." I smoothed my dress down as I stood, my unease growing with every passing second.

The sooner we got out of there, the better I would feel. Seeing Javier and my boss left me uneasy. Not to mention it tainted the perfect evening we had been enjoying until that point, though Alex didn't seem nearly as bothered by them being there. Then again, he didn't know about my interaction with them earlier that week.

"This was a beautiful first date." The door slammed as Alex climbed in behind the steering wheel.

"It was." He smiled, his face lighting up as he glanced over at me.

We rode in silence as he made his way back into town. The moment he pulled into my driveway and cut the engine. I felt a smidgen of remorse that the date was already ending. Despite my apprehension about wanting to take things to the next level, I liked Alex. He was kind and easy on the eyes.

"Would you like to come inside for a cup of coffee?"

Alex smiled as he turned toward me.

"As much as I would like to, I want to back up and take things slow. I like you, Trina. I'd rather not mess it up by coming inside."

"How would coming inside mess things up?" I cocked my brow at him, feeling a mix of disappointment and curiosity.

"Because if I come inside, I'm going to want to fuck you, and you're not ready for that."

"Oh." I pursed my lips and glanced out the window, feeling a mix of relief and frustration. "I should go. Dinner was amazing, thank you."

My fingers latched on the door handle, but Alex stopped me.

"Wait."

Hopping from the car, he hurried to my side and tugged open the door. He stepped into the opening and tugged me to the edge of my seat.

"I need to do this."

His lips descended on mine, causing goosebumps to prickle across my skin. My body melted into his as he laid claim to my mouth. His groin rubbed between my legs, eliciting a groan of approval from my chest. Just as it heated up, he stepped back.

"Let me help you down."

I blinked, still caught up in the kiss. "Oh," my voice whispered in confusion as he eased out.

"Slow, Trina. That's all this is. I'll call you when I get home so we can plan date number two."

seven

CATARINA

I SAT beside Johnny's bedside writing down his most recent stats. He was improving, but still wasn't showing any signs of waking up. Looking at his broken body, I couldn't help but think of my family. This was the shit I walked away from—damaged people led to too much heartache.

"How's the patient?" Harley lifted his chart from my palms and glanced over the notes I'd made. "Seems he's making some improvements. I can't believe the police weren't able to get a good match on his fingerprints."

"Well," I glanced to where his hands laid bound in gauze, "They're pretty fucked up."

"Speaking of fucked up," Harley shoved his chart into the cradle on the wall and followed me out into the hallway. "How's the hot detective?"

Alex and I had been out on a few dates in the last two weeks, but I was still hesitant to take things further. "Good. We're taking things slowly."

"I say you should just jump his bones."

Shaking my head, "How about we finish this shift so I can meet him up later… and who knows. Maybe I will."

I stood by the window in John Doe's room, my eyes lingering on the monitors that hummed softly, marking the passage of time with their rhythmic beeps. I was due to get off in an hour and wanted to check in on him more time. Despite the best efforts of the medical team, his condition remained unchanged. The mystery of who he was and what had happened to him weighed heavily on my mind.

A soft knock on the door pulled me from my thoughts. I turned to see Alex stepping into the room, his tall frame outlined against the hallway light. His expression was serious, but the moment he saw me, his face softened, and he offered a small smile.

"Hey, you," he greeted, his voice gentle. "Any progress?"

I shook my head. "No, nothing yet. He's stable, but… there's no improvement. It's like he's just stuck in limbo."

Alex nodded, his eyes moving over the monitors before settling on John Doe's pale face. "It's frustrating, isn't it? Knowing he's here, alive, but we can't do anything to bring him back. I wish we had more to go on."

"Yeah, me too," I said, my voice tinged with the weariness that I felt deep in my bones.

There was a brief silence between us as we both stared at the unconscious man, lost in our own thoughts. Then, Alex turned back to me, his expression brightening. "You still good for tonight?"

"Of course, you?" I bit down on my lip. "If you need to cancel on me, I understand."

Alex moved in front of me, "I'll be downstairs at eight." He pressed a chaste kiss to my cheek and stepped back. "See you later beautiful."

I lingered for a moment, feeling a strange mix of relief and lingering unease as I glanced back at John Doe. Something about the whole situation didn't sit right with me, but I couldn't quite put my finger on it.

Pushing those thoughts aside, I gathered my things and headed out, making my way down the long corridor. I was halfway to the locker room when I almost collided with Dr. Brooks and Javier Costa. They seemed to appear out of nowhere, their sudden presence startling me.

"Oh, sorry," I murmured, stepping back to let them pass.

But instead of moving on, Mr. Costa stopped; His cold, dark eyes were fixated on me. There was something predatory in his gaze that made my skin crawl.

"Miss Trina," he said smoothly, his voice oily with a charm that felt as fake as it was unsettling. "I was just about to check in on the man in that room. Tell me, do you think he's going to make it?"

His question, though simple, sent a chill down my spine. I wasn't sure why, but the way he asked it—like he was assessing a piece of meat rather than a human being—made my stomach turn.

"I… I don't know," I replied, my voice sounding small and uncertain. "He's stable, but it's hard to say. We're doing everything we can."

Dr. Brooks, standing just behind Costa, watched me intently, his usually pleasant demeanor replaced by something colder, more calculating. The change was subtle but palpable, like the temperature had dropped several degrees in the hallway.

"I see," Costa said, his lips curling into a smile that didn't reach his eyes. "Let's hope for the best, shall we?"

There was nothing comforting in his words, nothing reassuring in the way he looked at me. It was as if he knew something I didn't, something that made me more of a pawn in whatever game he was playing. The realization made me feel exposed, vulnerable, and I had to suppress the urge to shiver.

"Of course," I managed to say, forcing a polite smile. "If you'll excuse me, I need to clock out."

"Certainly," Costa replied, still smiling that unnerving smile. "We won't keep you."

I nodded and quickly walked past them, feeling their eyes on my back as I went. The encounter left a heavy weight in my chest, a nagging sense of dread that I couldn't shake. Something was wrong—deeply wrong—but I didn't know what, and that scared me more than I wanted to admit.

By the time I reached the locker room, I was practically trembling. I leaned against one of the lockers, taking a few deep breaths to steady myself. It was just nerves, I told myself. It had been a long day, and I was letting my imagination run wild. *There was nothing sinister about Dr. Brooks or Mr. Costa. They were just concerned about John Doe, just like everyone else. Right?*

I shook off the feeling as best I could and quickly changed out of my scrubs. I had a date with Alex, and I wasn't going to let the two of them ruin it.

When I finally stepped out of the hospital and into the cool evening air, I felt a little better. I spotted Alex waiting for me by his car, and the sight of him began to calm the storm of unease that had been brewing inside me.

"God, you look beautiful." He pulled me into his arms and pressed his lips to mine. "Come, let's go before I decide taking things slow is stupid."

I laughed as I climbed into his car. "Hey, can I ask you a question?"

"Sure," He put the car in reverse and backed out.

"That guy, Costa." I twisted my fingers in my lap. "Why do you want to put him in jail?"

Alex snorted, "He's a piece of shit. That man is suspected of being in the cartel—of supplying drugs and women to whoever has the fattest wallet."

"Why would he be with Dr. Brooks?"

"That is the million-dollar question." He pulled the car into a local tavern. "You hungry?"

"Famished."

Dinner with Alex was exactly what I needed—a simple, cozy affair at a little Italian place we'd found by chance. The food was rich and comforting, the kind that makes you forget the world outside for a little while. We laughed over shared stories, the tension of the day slowly unwinding with each glass of wine. Alex had a way of making everything feel lighter, like the weight I'd been carrying around all day wasn't so heavy after all. After dinner, we strolled through the nearby park, the night air cool against my skin, our conversation drifting from work to dreams, from jokes to deeper things that made me realize how much I appreciated his company. When it was time to go home, the drive was quiet, but it wasn't awkward—just peaceful. The streetlights flickered by, casting soft shadows across his face as he drove, and I found myself stealing glances at him, feeling a warmth in my chest that was both comforting and a little scary.

As he pulled up in front of my place, he turned to me with that easy smile of his, "I had a great time tonight."

"Come inside." I laced my fingers with his.

Alex shook his head, "As much as I want to do just that, I was serious, Trina. I want to take this slow—do things right. So, I'm going to walk you to that door, pull you close, kiss the hell out of you and then walk away. Because this—" He pointed his finger between us. "Is something I want to last."

"Okay." I smiled, his words washing over me like something real and meaningful.

Alex walked me to my door and did exactly what he promised before running to his truck. I watched in a daze as he reversed out of my driveway and waved. More conflicted than I ever had been, I pushed inside my home. My mind was a muddled mess of emotions.

Completely stuck in my head, I didn't notice the danger waiting for me inside.

CATARINA

IT HAPPENED the moment I stepped through the threshold and closed the door. He came out of nowhere, his hand wrapping around my neck and covering my mouth.

"Don't scream or you're dead." The putrid smell of his breath and stale cigarettes laced his heavy Spanish accent.

He had to be here because of Javier. I wasn't stupid enough to believe he was only trying to scare me. Men like Javier didn't leave witnesses behind. I flailed my arms, trying to loosen his grip, but he was a big guy and manhandled me with ease. My heels scraped across the floor as he pulled me into the kitchen. He punched me in the side, and a muffled cry escaped me.

"You've pissed off the wrong man," he grunted. "Now you're going to disappear."

He tugged me against his sturdy frame and tried to haul me toward the back door. I knew if he got me out of the house, I wouldn't live to see another day. I wiggled and squirmed, desperate for him to let go. My mouth managed to open enough to bite down on the flesh of his arm, causing him to tighten his grip even further. His forearm dug into my windpipe, threatening to cut off my air supply. I gasped as my nails instinctively started tearing at his skin, trying to get free. He tore at my hair, nearly ripping it from the root. It felt as though I could sense every nerve ending in my body individually. I fought to keep the tears at bay, knowing there was no time to be weak.

My hands reached out for the counter, latching onto the edge in an effort to break free. He hit me again, but I wasn't going without a fight—I couldn't. Just as I lost hold, my hand brushed a butcher knife. My fingers wrapped around the wooden handle as I yanked it from the surface. Everything my father and brothers had taught me came rushing back.

I knew the moment the blade entered his thick hide. He let out a grunt, swearing in Spanish as he let go of my body, and the knife slipped free. Instinct kicked in and I turned him into the prey. I jolted forward, pushing the pointed metal into his gut. We toppled over together, me landing on top of him, the knife held fast in my palm. His eyes widened with shock. He was not expecting me to best him.

"Fuck you." I pulled my arm back and plunged the knife back in. The sickening sounds of squishing resounded in the room as blood poured out around the stainless steel now tinted red.

He never had a chance to respond. His breathing became strained as he struggled for air. I scrambled backward, my back slamming against the cabinets. The blade dropped from my hands as I sat watching him take his last breath. I'd never killed a man before. That was my brothers—not me. But as his eyes glazed over and became hollow, I realized I'd become the person I had been desperately trying to avoid.

For a moment, the room was eerily silent, save for the labored gurgling of his final breaths. My heart pounded in my ears, and my body trembled with the adrenaline still coursing through me. I had to think quickly. I had to get rid of the body and clean up the mess before anyone found out. I couldn't let Alex, or anyone else, discover this side of me.

The side that knew how to kill.

His blood stained the floor and covered my skin. I sat staring at his still form for what felt like an eternity until my cell phone, which had fallen on the floor during our struggle, rattled across the floor. I cut my eyes to the offending object bouncing against the wood and slowly scooted toward it.

Alex was calling me. Knowing he would probably worry if I didn't answer, I dried my bloody hand on the rumpled dress I was wearing and answered.

"Hey." I forced my voice to relax.

"I'm home."

"Okay." It came out a bit more sarcastic than I wanted.

"Date two. Remember? I said I'd call so we could plan it."

"Right. Sorry, I was just about to grab a shower. Yes, let's plan something." My eyes strayed to the corpse bleeding out on my hardwoods. "Text me when you're free, and I'll check my work schedule and let you know."

Alex got quiet on the other end. "Are you having second thoughts?"

No. I'm just staring at a man I just killed.

"Absolutely not. I guess I'm just tired. How about I shower and call you back? Then we can decide when and what?"

"If you're sure." He seemed hesitant.

"I'm sure."

Sure, there is a dead man in my kitchen, and I can't tell you because you're a cop.

The internal war was raging inside me. I should have told him I had changed my mind, but the selfish part of me wanted to hang on to the normal he gave me, not the fucked-up life I was staring at.

"All right. Call me when you're done."

"Talk to you soon. Thanks for tonight, Alex."

Even if it ended with me shoving a knife into one of Javier Costa's men.

I gripped the phone in my hand after disconnecting. Right now, the only matter I needed to concern myself with was the dead man lying three feet from where I sat. The logical thing would have been to call Alex back and tell him what I'd done, but in doing that, I would have to tell him who I really was. Not to mention I'd be painting an even bigger target on myself—and possibly get him killed.

I was unable to take my eyes off the carnage lying before me. A large stream of blood clung to the fabric of his shirt as it oozed beneath his back. There was only one thing I could do. One person I could call. It didn't matter how hard I tried to reinvent myself, the fate of being an Anastasi would always catch up to me. Sitting there with the silent reminder of who I was, I knew there was no more running. It had found me—even if by coincidence, the underbelly of society had sucked me in.

I loosened the grip on my phone and stared at the darkened screen as if it was the talisman of death. Once I pressed the button, there was no going back to what I'd been working hard to create in this small town.

Small town.

I had to laugh at the thought. I'd come here because of the simplicity of the town. It was small, but still filled with enough life that I wouldn't get bored. It was the total opposite of Vegas—yet, here I sat, drenched in blood and anxiety. I pressed my eyes closed and took a calming breath. A tendril of panic wormed its way into my chest. What if he didn't answer? And if he did, what if he refused to help?

I couldn't think about that. He was my only hope. I swiped the screen alive, willing it to breathe life into the room. The number I'd refused to delete mocked me from my contacts, as though the inanimate writing was laughing at me beneath the thin glass screen.

Pressing the cellphone against my cheek, I held my breath and waited. For a moment, the air seized in my lungs when the familiar voice filtered through the line.

"Hello?"

I couldn't speak. The words fell dead on my tongue.

"Look." His irritation laced his tone. "I know someone's there… I can hear you breathing."

I drew in a stuttered gasp and swallowed. This was the moment everything would change. The past would collide with my future, blurring the lines I'd meticulously drawn out for myself. Lines that were being blown to smithereens with three words.

"I'm in trouble."

CATARINA

I DON'T KNOW how long I sat there staring at the corpse of the man who'd tried to kidnap me. It felt like hours—reality was, it probably had been. The unknown assailant was beginning to change color, his skin becoming an ashen blue. Even though his grotesque stare seemed to mock me, I couldn't move.

This is what I'd been trying to avoid—the death and carnage that seemed to follow my family was like a disease for which there was no cure. It didn't matter if I wanted a normal life. Being an Anastasi meant normal was crime and murder. Lost in the morbid vision I was trapped in, I didn't hear the door.

Strong hands gripped my face, turning my head from the dead body.

"Cat." His voice washed over me, snapping me from the dark thoughts. "Are you hurt?"

Unable to move or even force the answer out, I blinked. He looked just as I remembered, only his face held an expression I couldn't discern.

"You're in shock." The feeling of him sweeping me into his arms was something I hadn't realized I'd been longing for. "I'm going to get you cleaned up."

He didn't ask who the dead man was, didn't ask why I'd killed him. The only thing he did was tend to my state of despair. He set me on the toilet while he turned on the shower. The look in his eyes as he kneeled before me spoke of love.

"I'm going to undress you." Tugging the dress over my head, he sucked in a breath. "*Cuore mio.*" My heart. His palms brushed across the bruises covering my body and neck. "He did this?" He eased my bra off, leaving me in only my panties, and helped me stand.

I nodded, my eyes squeezing shut to stave off the tears finally threatening to fall. I'd come close to death. The thought made me shudder.

"Are you okay for a minute?"

Nodding absently, I watched as he stepped back and disrobed. Stunned, I couldn't take my eyes off him. This man had dropped everything to be here, even though I'd run away without so much as a goodbye.

"Donny." My voice wavered, the tears burning a trail down my skin.

"I'm here, Catarina." He wrapped my body in his arms and held me against his naked flesh. "I'll fix this for you. I promise."

"I don't deserve your help." I hiccuped through the sob that finally bubbled to the surface.

"You deserve the world." He lifted me and stepped our entwined bodies into the glass enclosure. The heat enveloped my senses as he held me beneath the spray and set me on my feet. "Let's get you cleaned off."

The water cascaded over us, mixing with the tears streaming down my face. Donny's hands were gentle but firm as he washed away the blood and grime from my skin. Each touch was a reassurance, a promise that he was there, that I wasn't alone.

As he rinsed the soap from my body, his eyes never left mine. The intensity of his gaze was almost too much to bear. It was filled with concern, love, and something deeper—a determination to protect me, no matter the cost.

"Why did you come?" I whispered. My voice was barely audible over the sound of the water.

"I came because you needed me," he replied, his voice steady. "And because I promised I'd always be there for you."

"But I ran away," I choked out, the guilt overwhelming. "I didn't even say goodbye."

"I know," he said softly. "Bu I'm here now, and that's all that matters."

"Do my brothers know?" My voice cracked with uncertainty.

"No, but I'll need to make some phone calls to get the dead body out of your kitchen. Can you tell me what happened?" He caressed my shoulders.

"I don't know what to do," I admitted, my voice trembling. "I killed him, Donny. I didn't mean to, but I did."

"He was going to take you," Donny said firmly. "You did what you had to do to survive. Do you know why he would be here?"

"I overheard something at the hospital between one of the doctors and a man. I found out tonight while at dinner, the man I saw him with is being investigated for drugs or something."

"Who told you that?" Donny cut off the water and stepped out. He wrapped a towel around his waist, then held one open for me.

"A friend." He wrapped the cotton towel around my body.

"Elaborate. What kind of friend, Catarina?" Donny folded his arms across his chest and pinned me with a knowing glare.

"Look, Donny." I turned and walked into the bedroom. "I came here to start over. So, yes, I was on a date. A date that ended in my killing a man in my kitchen, so it's safe to say, a second date won't be happening." I grabbed a pair of leggings and a tank top. Donny watched as I slipped the material over my naked body.

"Why not? I'm here to fix your problem."

"Because he's a cop. I don't think lying to him is the best way to start a relationship." I dropped onto the bed and sighed. "It was doomed before tonight, anyway. He doesn't know who I am. No one here does."

Donny moved in front of me, the towel tucked tightly around his hips.

"Is that the only reason?"

My eyes tracked his nearly naked body as I scanned the expanse of his defined chest and landed on his eyes. It wasn't the only reason, but if I told him why I couldn't be with someone else, he would never leave.

"Did you stop loving me, Catarina? Is that it?"

His words struck my heart hard, causing me to inhale sharply.

"Loving you is exactly why I ran. The life you live—the life my family lives—isn't what I want."

"You're an Anastasi. It's not something you can run from, *cuore mio*." Donny grabbed his boxers and pants, tugging them over his hips.

My head fell with his words. He was right. No matter how hard I tried to separate myself from who I was, I couldn't. The blood-stained hardwoods were proof of that. Not only that, but the very man I had tried to eradicate from my system was the first person I called. What did that say about me? I looked up to find his eyes boring into me.

"I didn't mean for this to happen." The tears began to fall again.

"I know, but even the purest of intentions can become deadly. Wait here. I'm going to make a few calls and try to clean up the mess."

My eyes trailed his naked back as he left the room. It was then I noticed the time. How I wasn't dead on my feet was a miracle. It was almost three in the morning, and I had no desire to sleep. It was a good thing I didn't have to work until tomorrow night. I wasn't sure I would've made it if I'd had a morning shift. I tugged my hair into a ponytail and headed into the living room. Donny was on his phone with his back to me. Like a moth to a flame, I moved behind him and pressed my palm to the muscles flexing as he talked.

He turned, his eyes searching me for something. I glanced away, confused at my reaction to the man I had run from, which was a mistake. They landed on the reminder of why Donny was here. My breath hitched, and my vision blurred. Strong hands wrapped around me and lifted me from the floor.

"I told you to wait." Donny moved down the hall and laid me on the bed. "Some guys will be here in a few hours to dispose of his body. Until then, we'll stay in here."

Donny pulled back the covers and shifted me beneath them. He wordlessly moved around to the opposite side and slipped in beside me—but not before stripping off his pants. My eyes zeroed in on the fitted boxers he wore, sending a jolt of need through me. Guilt ransacked me, knowing that not even six hours earlier I was with another man.

"Stop thinking, Cat. I'm here, and I'm not leaving."

He wrapped his arm around me and tugged me against his chest. As though I was meant for him, my body fit perfectly in the curve of his form. His fingers brushed against my hip, trailing a blaze of fire in their wake. Closing my eyes, I gave in to the feeling of being safe wrapped in him. Tomorrow, reality would crash down on me as my calm, blissful life imploded. I still had to face the fact a man had tried to kill me, and that it wasn't likely the last attempt.

It wasn't long before my eyes grew heavy, and I gave in to the sensation of Donny's warmth. Sleep claimed me, sucking me into the dark expanse of the faceless man lying on my kitchen floor. Every time I wanted to scream out, Donny's voice filled my nightmare, constantly calling me back and anchoring me to the present.

DONNY

I SLIPPED OUT of bed once I was certain her nightmares had stopped. She'd run from one darkness only to land in another. Only this time, I wasn't sure what evil was hunting her. She had no idea the danger was gone in Vegas. Vincenzo and Matias Silva had found Ivanov in Chile and delved out a decent amount of revenge on him. He was the reason her life had been in upheaval. Hell, it'd been the reason the entire family had been in turmoil. But she ran, leaving no trace or way to find her.

Until now.

I couldn't say I hadn't tried to find her. Massimo had given me his blessing to leave Vegas. He knew how I felt about her. He'd always known. We were best friends, and nothing got past him. When he assigned me to protect her, I knew my battle to stay away from her would be lost. The moment my lips touched hers all those months ago, I knew she would be mine.

A few of the guys came without asking questions. I informed them not to breathe a word to Massimo about why they'd come. It was my job to tell him I'd found her—and I would as soon as I knew what the hell she'd gotten herself into. Most of the morning was spent searching the internet for this man she called Javier Costa. When I couldn't get what I needed, I reached out to Alec. He was our go-to guy for digging up information on someone. And like the goons who'd disposed of the piece of shit's body, he would keep my location a secret.

My eyes shifted to the sound of feet padding across the floor to find Catarina standing in the doorway of the kitchen. Her eyes were glued to the hardwood floor.

"It's cleaned up. There is no trace of the monster Javier sent here." I held her gaze.

"Okay." She moved to the table and sat down. "When will you be leaving?"

"Leaving?" I scoffed.

"Yes. I am trying to make a life here, Donny. A life that isn't that of an Anastasi."

My body moved of its own accord, and I knelt before her.

"I told you last night, I'm not leaving you. If that means I stay here in this Podunk town, then so be it. A man tried to kill you, Cat. I won't leave you unprotected."

She held her tongue, mulling over my words. "I have to work tonight."

"Call in sick." I stood and moved to the counter, knowing she would blow up.

"No." The sound of the chair scraping across the floor told me I was right. "I will not call in sick, so you can forget that."

"The man who tried to kill you is likely linked to your boss. Do you think it's wise to show your face there today?"

"I don't—" The sound of her phone cut her words off. Her eyes shot to the device incessantly ringing against the counter. She grabbed it and stared at the screen, conflicted about whether to answer. I knew by her body language it was him—the man she'd been out on a date with.

"Go ahead, answer it." I barked, my jealousy rearing its ugly head.

She stabbed her finger at the button and pressed the phone to her ear.

"Hello."

Her skin slowly tinged pink as she watched me for my reaction. My body tensed as I listened to a one-sided conversation. It didn't take a rocket scientist to know he was talking about their time together and probably asking for more.

"Alex, I had fun last night, but like I told you. I'm just not ready. I'm sorry if I led you on."

Her words made my heart soar. She might have wanted to create a new life here, but her heart still belonged to me. I was going to remind her of that as soon as she hung up the phone. I inched closer to her, watching as her throat bobbed with nerves. My close proximity was making her body flush, and her pupils dilate.

"I'll see you at the hospital tonight. I'm sorry again. Yes, of course, we can be friends." I crowded her against the counter, pressing my body against hers. "Alex, I have to go."

I grabbed the phone and disconnected the call. The phone clattered against the hard surface as I tossed it to the side.

"What are you doing?" Her voice came out a whisper.

"Did he touch you?" I ran my fingers down her arms, tracing the ink that covered her skin.

"Donny." She whimpered.

"Answer me, Catarina. Did…Alex have his hands on you?"

"We didn't have sex if that's what you're asking me. I couldn't."

I thrust my hips, pressing my arousal into her center. She hissed as her eyes closed. "Say it."

"I COULDN'T. OKAY? IS THAT WHAT YOU WANT TO HEAR? THAT I couldn't sleep with a man who wanted me."

"And why do you think that is?" Fisting her hair, I tilted her head backward and dipped my mouth to the spot I knew drove her wild with want.

"I…" She moaned as I latched onto her neck, sucking the tender flesh into my mouth.

"Tell me." My tongue traced a path to her ear.

"You're the only man I've ever been with. The only man I'll ever want."

I froze at her admission.

"What do you mean? Are you saying I was the first man to touch you, Catarina?"

"The first and only." Her words came out in a whisper, but I didn't miss what she grumbled next. "And you've ruined me for all others."

All control I had went out the window as I fastened my mouth over hers. My tongue delved between her lips, owning her with everything I had to give. A slow sizzle started in my blood, igniting into a full-blown inferno as I staked my claim. Catarina moaned against my lips, giving in to the passion that burned between us. Heat coursed through me, incinerating me from the inside out. I needed this woman almost as much as I needed air to breathe.

Lifting her from the floor, I set her on the counter and wedged myself between her thighs. The heat of her center radiated against my groin, breathing life into my already hard cock. My palms pressed against the counter as I leaned into her body.

"And that's how it will remain, Catarina. No other man will touch you. No other man will have what belongs to me. This. Is. Mine." My hips ground into the space between her legs as I said each word.

Catarina narrowed her eyes, her mind at war with her body. Her lashes fluttered as her lids closed.

"Donny," she whispered, the tone laced with desire and apprehension.

My mouth fastened over hers again, taking what belonged to me. She resisted for a fraction of a second before her lips finally parted, welcoming me inside and giving in to her body's demands. The touch of her hands against my shoulders sent electric currents of need through my veins. This woman was going to be my undoing. I'd known that from the moment I met her. In all the years before, trying to erase her from my mind with meaningless sex, Catarina had always burned in the depths of my soul—owning me from the inside out.

"What are you doing?" she whimpered, her legs latching around my back as I broke the kiss and pulled her off the counter into my arms.

"Reminding you why you're mine." I navigated us to her bedroom and tossed her onto the bed.

I stripped my clothes, leaving me naked before her. Her eyes widened as I stalked forward and tugged her legs to the edge of the bed. In one sweep, I removed her leggings and panties, tossing them to the floor.

"This is mine."

I dipped my finger between her folds as I stroked my cock. She moaned, her body arching beneath my touch. My knees hit the floor as I shoved her legs apart and pressed my face to her center. My mind blanked the moment I tasted her sweet flavor. It'd been too long since I'd had her essence on my tongue. Every swipe across her nub had her body tensing and her legs tightening around my head. With determination, I inserted a finger and pressed it against the soft ridge inside her. Catarina exploded, her walls clamping down around my digit. Her release flooded my mouth, filling me with the flavor I craved. Kissing up her thigh, I climbed onto the bed. Her tank top easily ripped down the center as I yanked it from her flesh.

"Donny," she whimpered my name as my mouth closed around her taut pink bud. I spent time teasing and biting her nipple, taking time with each breast. "Please." Her plea had my cock pulsing—no, demanding to be buried in her warm cavern.

I didn't need any more encouragement. I pushed to my feet and fisted my shaft. After moving between her legs, I guided myself into her warm center. She let out a long groan of approval as I seated fully inside her. Catarina dug her nails into my back, the tips biting my flesh as I rocked into her. If there was one thing Catarina and I did well together, it was this. God had made her body for mine. We fit together perfectly, making our union explosive. I could feel her in every fiber of my being. With each thrust, my blood heated with a fire only she could extinguish.

My movements grew into a steady rhythm, causing her core to tighten around me. Grinding my pelvis against her, Catarina erupted. Her cries of release filled the room as her walls clamped on my shaft. The tight feeling of her pussy convulsing around my cock caused me to follow her over the edge. My orgasm ripped through me, cum erupting from my shaft and filling her womb. I wanted to mark her as mine in the most primal sense, leaving no confusion in her mind who she belonged to.

Breathing heavily, I collapsed beside her, pulling her close into my arms. Her skin was flushed, her breath still coming in shallow gasps as she nestled against my chest.

"Donny," she whispered, her voice tinged with a mix of contentment and lingering uncertainty.

"I'm here, Cat," I murmured, stroking her hair. "I'm not going anywhere."

"I'm scared," she admitted, her fingers tracing circles on my chest. "Everything is so complicated. I don't know how to deal with it."

"No more running. No more hiding. We'll figure it out."

She nodded, her body relaxing slightly against mine. For the first time in what felt like forever, I felt a sense of peace. Catarina was back in my arms where she belonged, and I was determined to protect her, no matter what.

After this, I would belong to her, just as she did to me—only this time, it was forever.

eleven

CATARINA

AS SOON AS I stepped out of the shower, a cold wave of regret washed over me, sharper than the water droplets still clinging to my skin. Sleeping with Donny had been an error in judgment, a fleeting moment of weakness where desire drowned out reason. He was everything I wanted—dark, dangerous, and irresistibly magnetic—but nothing I needed or should have allowed myself to have. With Donny, bloodshed was never far behind, like a shadow that lurked just out of sight but always present. And this time, the blood on my hands wasn't his doing. It was mine, a consequence of my own reckless choices. The thought gnawed at me as I dried myself off, my movements mechanical and devoid of purpose.

MY HEART LURCHED IN MY CHEST WHEN I SAW HIM LEANING casually against my front door as if he belonged there, as if he belonged anywhere in my life. But the truth was, he didn't, and I knew it. Yet here he was, his presence a dark cloud over my already tumultuous thoughts.

"No, Donny," I said, waving my hands in the air in a futile attempt to clear the thick tension that filled the room. "How in the hell am I going to explain why you're at work with me?" My voice wavered, betraying the panic bubbling just beneath the surface.

"I don't care," he replied, his tone resolute and unyielding, like the man himself. "But you're not going without me."

I let out an exasperated sigh, stomping around him in a bid to reach the door, my mind racing for solutions that wouldn't come. But the door wouldn't budge, as if the universe itself was conspiring against me.

"Fuck," I muttered, frustration boiling over as I fisted my hair and screamed, the sound raw and primal. I could feel my sanity slipping through my fingers like sand. "Fine. I have to work, so let's go. I'll figure something out when we get there."

Donny didn't say a word, just stepped aside, and opened the door, his expression unreadable. I hurried down the steps, my feet barely touching the ground as I turned toward the hospital, desperate to escape the suffocating atmosphere he brought with him.

"What the fuck are you doing?" His hand clamped down on my arm, halting me mid-stride, his grip firm but not painful. Yet.

"Walking to work like I usually do," I snapped, yanking my arm out of his grasp, my heart pounding in my chest.

"No, it's not safe. I'll drive," he declared, his voice leaving no room for argument as he half-dragged me to his truck, his grip like a vice that wouldn't let go. He jerked open the door with a force that made the metal groan in protest. "Get in."

Knowing full well that defiance was futile, I climbed inside, letting out a frustrated huff as I settled into the seat. I didn't have the energy to fight him, not when the weight of my own mistakes was already crushing me. Donny climbed behind the steering wheel, but instead of starting the engine, he turned toward me, his dark eyes boring into mine with an intensity that made my breath catch. Before I could react, his hands were on me, dragging me into his lap, his mouth crashing down on mine with a ferocity that sent my mind spiraling.

This man was my kryptonite, my downfall, and in that moment, I was helpless to resist him. But the reality of the situation hit me like a freight train, and I shoved him back, scrambling to move back into my seat.

"Stop," I managed to say, my voice trembling with the effort to regain control. "You can't do that, Donny. And another thing…" I took a deep breath, steeling myself for what I knew would set him off. "You can't call me Catarina at work. No one here knows me by that name."

His jaw ticked, his expression darkening as he pinned me with a glare that made my stomach twist into knots.

"What do they know you by?" His voice was low, dangerous, like the calm before a storm.

"Trina Aniston," I confessed, my head dropping in shame. The guilt of the lie weighed heavily on me, pressing down until I could barely breathe.

"Trina." He spat the name like it was poison on his tongue, his disgust palpable. "Fine then, Trina. Anything else I should know?"

"They think I'm from out east," I added, my voice small, barely audible over the thundering of my heart.

"Right. East," he echoed, the word dripping with sarcasm as he started the engine, the roar of the truck masking the silence that fell between us.

Donny backed out of the driveway with a tense silence hanging in the air between us, the weight of unspoken words pressing down like a heavy fog. The short drive to the hospital felt like an eternity, my mind racing with the million ways this day could go wrong. When we finally parked, I hesitated, my hand lingering on the door handle as if the simple act of opening it would somehow commit me to the chaos I feared was waiting inside. But there was no turning back now.

We climbed out of the truck, the morning air cool against my skin, doing little to soothe the anxiety twisting in my gut. Donny's presence at my side was both a comfort and a threat, a double-edged sword I wasn't sure how to handle. As we entered the hospital, my thoughts swirled with dread.

Harley was sitting behind the nurse's station when we reached my floor, her bright personality a stark contrast to the storm brewing inside me. As soon as she caught sight of Donny, her eyes widened, a mischievous smile tugging at the corners of her lips.

"Uh…hey, Trina." Harley's gaze flicked between Donny and me. Her curiosity was evident. But when her eyes settled on the faint bruises I'd tried to hide with makeup, concern flashed across her face before she quickly masked it. "Who's this hunk of a man?"

I sighed inwardly. Of course, Harley wouldn't hold back. She never did. She had no filter, and her words often tumbled out without a second thought. Given Donny's rugged good looks, I should have expected her reaction. Lord knows, my own eyes were drawn to him more often than I cared to admit.

"This is Donny. A—" I hesitated. My mind was scrambling for the right word to describe the man who turned my world upside down in more ways than one. "Friend from home. He's visiting for a few days and wanted to see where I worked. Is that okay?"

Harley's eyes sparkled with interest as she glanced back at Donny, clearly amused by the situation. "As long as he stays out of patient rooms, I don't have an issue." She shot him a playful wink that made my blood simmer with irritation. "He can keep me company when you're in with Johnny."

I bit back a scowl at her blatant flirtation. The last thing I needed was Harley encouraging Donny, especially when I was barely holding it together. I shifted the conversation quickly, hoping to steer it away from dangerous territory. "Any change?" I asked, my voice tinged with a desperation I couldn't quite hide. I needed something good to happen, something to distract me from the train wreck my life had become.

Harley shook her head, her smile dimming slightly. "Nope. Still no change."

Before I could respond, the phone at the nurse's desk rang, saving me from further scrutiny. Harley answered it, giving me the perfect opportunity to escape.

Donny followed me into the staff room, his eyes tracking my every move as I put away my belongings. The tension between us was palpable, a thick cord ready to snap at any moment. I grabbed my stethoscope, trying to focus on the task at hand. I needed to see Johnny—John Doe, as we called him. I hadn't checked on him in a few days, and for some inexplicable reason, the stranger in the bed gave me a sense of comfort I couldn't find anywhere else.

"Wait out here. I'll be out in a minute." I pointed to the wall outside Johnny's room, hoping Donny would respect my request and stay put. But before I could take another step, he pushed past me, storming into the room as if he owned the place.

"What the fuck?" I hissed, hurrying in after him, my heart pounding with a mix of anger and fear. "Donny, you can't be in here. Are you trying to get me fired?"

He stopped at the foot of Johnny's bed. His gaze was fixed on the unconscious man as if seeing a ghost. His reaction sent a chill down my spine, the air in the room suddenly thick with unspoken tension.

"Catarina… please tell me you aren't that damn oblivious," Donny snarled, his voice laced with frustration as he yanked his arm out of my grasp and raked his fingers through his hair in agitation.

His words stung, a sharp slap to my already frayed nerves. "Excuse me?" I snapped, taking a step back, my anger flaring like a wildfire. "Get the fuck out," I growled, my voice trembling with the effort to keep my emotions in check.

Donny didn't budge, his eyes never leaving Johnny's face. "Don't you know who this is?" He closed his eyes, pinching the bridge of his nose as if trying to ward off a headache. He mumbled something under his breath, words I couldn't quite catch but felt the weight of, nonetheless.

"No. That's why we call him John Doe, you jackass," I retorted, my voice dripping with sarcasm as I moved to the bedside. I focused on checking Johnny's fluids, anything to keep my hands from shaking. "He was here before I was. His bandages just came off, and as you can see, he's still swollen and bruised. Alex… rather Detective Coulter, hasn't been able to ID him. It's as though he doesn't exist."

The words hung in the air between us, heavy with implication. Donny's reaction, the tension in his body, the way he looked at Johnny—it all pointed to something I wasn't ready to face. But I couldn't ignore it anymore, not with the way my heart was pounding in my chest, telling me that everything was about to change.

"He won't be able to identify him," Donny murmured, stepping closer to the bed, his eyes narrowing as he examined the unconscious man more intently.

"I'm afraid that's true," I replied, my voice barely above a whisper as I processed the implications. "Pretty sure he was beaten and dumped. Alex seems to think he was involved with Javier's dealings and should be dead."

"He wasn't. And his identity was scrubbed to protect him," Donny's voice was low, grim, and filled with a certainty that sent a shiver down my spine.

"He wasn't what? And how could you possibly know that about his identity?" I stared at him, confused, trying to piece together the puzzle that had just taken a sharp, unexpected turn. "Not everyone operates like my family, Donny."

Donny's eyes softened, and the hard edge that he usually carried with him seemed to melt away, revealing a vulnerability I'd rarely seen. "Look at him, Cat. Really look at him."

I turned back to the unconscious man I'd come to care about, my eyes tracing the contours of his face, still bruised, and swollen but unmistakably familiar. For the first time, I saw beyond the injuries, beyond the trauma, and a strange sense of recognition washed over me. It was like seeing someone from a dream, someone you knew but couldn't quite place.

"He wasn't involved with Javier." Donny leaned down. His breath was warm against my ear as he whispered the words that shattered the fragile reality I'd been clinging to. "The man who put him in this bed was Dmitri Ivanov."

My hands flew to my mouth as a gasp escaped my lips, the sound echoing in the silent room. How could I have missed this? How had

I not known? All this time, the man I'd been tending to, the man I'd shared my nights with in quiet conversation, was someone I should have recognized. Someone who meant everything to my brother. A lone tear slipped down my cheek, a physical manifestation of the storm raging inside me. This was going to cause a shitstorm I wasn't ready for.

"I don't…" My voice broke as I reached out, my hand trembling as it brushed over Michael's still arm. "How is this possible?" I turned to Donny, searching his face for answers, for something that made sense in this twisted mess. He looked as stunned as I felt, though there was a flicker of relief in his eyes, as if a weight had been lifted off his shoulders. He'd been there, seen the pain and turmoil my family had endured, the pain I had run from. The guilt hit me like a freight train, a bitter reminder of the choices I had made.

"I have no idea," Donny admitted, his voice soft, almost gentle. "But you understand what this means, don't you?"

My head snapped back to the still form on the bed, my mind reeling from the implications. "No. You can't. Not yet."

"Catarina," Donny's voice was firm as he reached out, trying to place a comforting hand on my shoulder, but I flinched away, my emotions too raw. "You can't keep this secret. It's not fair to your family…or Antonio."

"We need to be sure. You could be wrong." The words felt hollow, even as I said them, because deep down, I knew they were a lie. The man lying there, the one I had been so desperate to save, was Michael. There was no denying it anymore.

But admitting that meant my new life, the sanctuary I'd built in this small town, was unraveling, coming to an end. It was selfish—I knew that—but the thought of calling my brothers, of facing the truth, filled me with a dread that I couldn't shake. My life had been built on a lie, and now that lie was staring me in the face from a hospital bed, waiting to tear everything apart.

"Excuse me." A voice cut through the thick tension in the room, startling me out of my spiraling thoughts.

I turned to find Alex standing in the doorway, his expression a mixture of surprise and suspicion as he took in the scene before him. His eyes narrowed at the sight of Donny, the question in his gaze unmistakable. I wasn't ready to answer it. Not yet.

"Alex," I forced a smile, trying to keep my voice steady despite the turmoil churning inside me. "I wasn't expecting you so soon."

"I was in the area and decided to come by sooner," Alex replied, his tone clipped as his eyes locked onto Donny with a sharp intensity. "I'm Detective Coulter. And you are?" He extended his hand toward Donny, the tension between them crackling like a live wire.

"He's my cousin," I blurted out, the words rushing out before I could think them through, desperate to defuse the situation.

Donny quirked an eyebrow at me, his smirk filled with amusement, clearly not intending to let the comment slide. "She's being shy," he drawled, the mischievous glint in his eyes making my stomach drop. "I'm her fiancé," he quipped, the lie slipping out as easily as breathing. "I know you and she have gone out a few times, but I'm back, and she's off limits," Donny growled, his voice low and possessive.

"Donny," I gasped, my cheeks flaming with a mix of anger and embarrassment. This was the last thing I needed. "Alex, can I talk to you in the hallway for a moment?" I shot Donny a pleading look, silently begging him to stop before things spiraled further out of control. My mind raced as I tried to come up with something, anything, that could keep this situation from exploding.

"Sure." Alex's voice was steady, but I could see the flicker of something—disappointment, perhaps—in his eyes. His gaze shifted between Donny and me, a silent question hanging in the air before he followed me out into the hall.

The moment we were alone, I turned to him, my heart heavy with the weight of what I had to say. "I'm so sorry. I should have told you from the start that I was just out of a relationship."

"Engaged," he corrected, his tone soft but firm.

"What?" I blinked, momentarily thrown off.

"You mean you were engaged. And now he's back." His words hung in the air like an accusation, though there was no anger behind them—just a quiet resignation.

"It's… complicated," I stammered, my hands twisting nervously as I tried to explain the mess I was in. "I don't want to go home, and he won't move here."

Alex's expression softened, but the sadness in his eyes was unmistakable. "Are you in love with him?" he asked, the question cutting straight to the heart of the matter.

"I…" I blew out a breath, searching for the right words. I couldn't lie, not to him. He deserved the truth, no matter how much it might hurt. "I don't think I'll ever not be in love with him. I just don't think we can be together. Like I said, it's—"

"Complicated," he finished for me, his voice gentle but tinged with sorrow. "Look. I like you a lot, but if you were mine, I'd be doing exactly what he's doing—fighting for you. If things don't work out, I'll be here to help pick up the pieces, even if it's just as your friend. But the way he looks at you…" Alex swallowed hard. His voice was thick with emotion. "I won't be the thing that comes between you two."

"Thank you." The sincerity of his words hit me like a punch to the gut. This man was more honorable, more selfless, than I could ever hope to be. "For what it's worth, I think I could have liked you back." I offered a small, bittersweet smile, wishing things could have been different. "Any luck on John Doe's identity?" I asked even though the answer no longer mattered in the way it once had. We both knew who lay in that hospital bed.

"No." Alex shook his head, his voice tinged with frustration. "I'm going to reach out to some more contacts. Let me know if he wakes up."

"I will." I hugged him, feeling a pang of guilt as I watched him walk away, heading toward the elevator. He was a good man, the kind of man who deserved better than the chaos that followed me. But my heart... my heart was tangled up with the one probably stewing inside the patient's room.

As soon as I stepped back into the room, the door slammed shut behind me. Donny was on me in an instant, his body pressing me against the wall with a force that made my breath hitch.

"Cousin?" His voice was low, dangerous, as he shoved his knee between my legs, the friction of his jeans against my scrubs igniting a fire in my veins. The sensation was maddening, a cruel reminder of the pull he had on me. "Does your cousin kiss you like this?" His mouth crashed down on mine, the kiss fierce, claiming, leaving me breathless and reeling.

When he finally pulled away, I could barely manage a whisper. "No," I admitted, my voice trembling with desire.

"Don't you forget it," Donny growled, his gaze burning into mine with an intensity that left me weak. He released me, stepping back as if to put distance between us and the temptation that simmered just beneath the surface. But the momentary reprieve was short-lived as his eyes flicked back to the unconscious man lying in the bed. "Now, we have to talk about this."

I swallowed hard, dread curling in my stomach like a snake. "What's there to talk about? We can't call Massimo yet. Not until we're sure."

"I'm sure, Catarina," Donny's voice was firm, unwavering, as he walked over to the bedside and cradled Michael's hand in his. The tenderness of the gesture was so at odds with the man I knew that it nearly broke me. "And the sooner you accept it, the sooner we can make the call."

I shook my head, my heart clenching at the thought of what would happen next. "They need to know Michael is alive."

I bit my lip, trying to hold back the tears that threatened to spill over. "Donny, I'm not ready. Everything will change—everything I've tried to build here. I'll lose it all."

He turned to face me, his expression softened with understanding, but there was a steely resolve in his eyes. "You won't lose me," he said quietly. "But you can't keep this from them. They deserve to know. Antonio deserves to know. And we owe it to Michael to make sure he's safe."

I nodded, finally letting the tears fall as the weight of the truth settled over me. There was no turning back now. The life I had tried to build, the sanctuary I had created, was unraveling before my eyes, and there was nothing I could do to stop it. "Okay," I whispered, my voice barely audible. "We'll call Massimo. But I need time—just a little more time."

Donny's expression softened even further, and he nodded, understanding what I was asking for. "I'll give you time, Cat. But not too much. This secret can't stay buried for long."

I nodded again, feeling a deep sense of loss even though I knew this was the right thing to do. Turning back to Michael, I reached out and gently touched his hand, feeling the warmth of his skin beneath my fingers. "Please wake up soon, Michael. We need you."

And with those words, I realized just how much we all did.

twelve

I SLUMPED into the chair beside Michael's bed, the weight of the revelation pressing down on me like a lead blanket. Knowing it was him changed everything. The room felt different now, heavy with a responsibility I wasn't sure I was ready to bear. I wasn't just his nurse anymore—I was the only family he had, and that realization made my insides churn with a mix of fear and indecision. Antonio and Mia deserved to know that Michael was alive, but I couldn't bring myself to make the call. Not yet. Donny had agreed to give me a few days, understanding the complexity of the situation, especially since the family didn't even know he had found me. The phone call I was dreading would be difficult in more ways than one, and I wasn't ready to face it.

"We need to deal with your boss, *cuore mio*." Donny's voice was soft as he ran his palm down the back of my head, his fingers gently twining in the strands of my ponytail.

Cuore mio—my heart. He'd called me that for as long as I could remember. Back when I was just his best friend's little sister, the nickname had been a mystery to me. We were only a few years apart in age, had practically grown up together, and he had always been the boy I couldn't have. As I got older and realized I didn't want to be part of the family business, I learned Donny was someone out of my reach. But despite all of that, my heart hadn't gotten the memo. He was the one constant in my life, the one person I could never let go, even when I knew I should.

I blew out a breath and stood, pushing away the emotions threatening to overwhelm me. "I need to make my rounds."

"Catarina." Donny's voice rumbled with a warning that made me pause.

"No." I turned to face him, pressing my hand against his chest, trying to convey with touch what I couldn't say out loud. "I have a job to do, and I won't let you get in the way of that. We will deal with Dr. Brooks later."

The door creaked open, and we both turned toward the sound. Harley stood in the doorway, her eyes flicking suspiciously between Donny and me. The look on her face told me she had questions, questions I wasn't ready to answer.

"Um… Dr. Brooks is looking for you," Harley announced, her voice tinged with unease.

The low growl of displeasure that came from Donny was unmistakable, and Harley's eyebrows shot up in surprise. She glanced at me with concern, clearly sensing the tension in the room.

"I'll go see him." I tried to move around Donny, but his hand shot out, wrapping firmly around my bicep.

"I don't like it," he whispered, his voice low but not low enough to keep Harley from hearing.

"Is there something I need to know about?" Harley asked, her tone shifting to one of authority as she planted her hands on her hips, effectively blocking the door.

"No." "Yes." Donny and I answered simultaneously, our voices overlapping in a way that only heightened the tension.

"Yes," Donny repeated, his eyes pleading with me to tell her the truth. "You need to tell her."

"I can't," I whispered, my voice breaking under the weight of the confession I wasn't ready to make. Telling Harley what had happened would mean admitting I'd lied about my identity, and I wasn't sure I could handle the fallout from that.

"Trina," Harley said, locking the door behind her and dropping her arms. "If you're worried about telling me who you are, don't be. I've known."

Her admission hit me like a punch to the gut, and I stumbled backward, my body colliding with the edge of the bed, jostling Michael's still form. "What?" I managed to choke out, my mind reeling. "I don't—"

Harley held up her hand, cutting me off before I could spiral further. "You came here with very little background information. Sure, your one reference spoke highly of you, and maybe the hospital board bought it. But…" she paused, a small smile playing at the corners of her lips, "I come from a military family and have a need to know everything about my environment. I knew you were hiding or running from something. So, is that it? You're in witness protection or something?"

Donny chuckled, a sound that sent a shiver down my spine. "Or something." He cocked an eyebrow at me, crossing his arms over his broad chest. The challenge in his eyes was unmistakable. "If you don't tell her, I will."

"Fine. Fuck." I clenched my fists, my nails digging into the soft flesh of my palms, grounding myself in the sharp pain. "What I'm about to tell you cannot leave this room, Harley. Do you understand?"

Harley's eyes darted between Donny and me, her expression nonchalant, but I could see the curiosity burning behind her gaze. "Okay," she answered casually, but I knew she was paying attention to every detail.

"No. I'm serious," I insisted, my voice dropping to a hard edge. "It could put you in danger. And you can't breathe a word to Alex. He of all people doesn't need to know."

"Because he's a cop?" she asked, her brows furrowing in confusion. "Aren't they supposed to know if someone is in witness protection?"

"Probably. But I'm not in witness protection," I said, shaking my head. The words felt heavy as they left my lips. "I changed my name and moved here because I didn't want to be associated with my family anymore."

Harley's body tensed, and I could see her mind racing, putting together the pieces of the puzzle. "Did they hurt you?" Her gaze flicked to Donny, eyes narrowing in suspicion. "Is that where the bruises came from? Did he give them to you?"

"No, he definitely did not give me these bruises." My fingers grazed over the tender skin around my throat, and I saw the concern deepen in Harley's eyes. Realization hit me like a ton of bricks—how foolish I had been to run from the very people who would die for me. "Donny, nor my family, would ever hurt me—not intentionally. But carnage seems to be part of the family business."

Harley's eyes were locked on mine, the weight of my words sinking in. "And Donny is here because…" she prompted, letting the question hang between us.

"It seems no matter how far I ran, trouble found me." Tears welled up in my eyes, blurring my vision. "I'm not from the east like I said. I'm from Vegas. My brothers run the family business there, and my father takes care of things in Sicily." I waited, letting my words sink in, knowing that Harley was smart enough to understand what I was implying.

"I see." Harley's gaze shifted to Donny, sizing him up with new understanding. "I assume you're more than a friend?"

"Yes. Catarina is mine, and I will do whatever it takes to protect her," Donny stated, his voice steady and filled with a quiet intensity that left no room for doubt.

"Yours?" Harley's eyes narrowed, but not with anger—more like she was trying to understand the depth of his words. "Like property?"

"No. Mine, as in the woman who I'd die for," Donny clarified, his voice softening but still firm.

Harley's eyes widened slightly, surprised by the depth of his declaration. "What about Alex?"

"He knows his place," Donny growled, the possessiveness in his tone unmistakable.

"What kind of trouble are you in… Catarina, was it?" Harley asked, her voice careful, as if she were piecing together the delicate threads of the story.

"Yes. My real name is Catarina Anastasi," I admitted, the weight of my true identity hanging heavily between us. "But I am really a nurse. I would never lie about my capabilities, especially if it put people in harm's way." My eyes drifted back to Michael, lying unconscious on the bed.

"You know him, don't you?" Harley's voice was soft, understanding.

"Yes, but I'm not ready to reveal that information yet. And honestly, we just realized it ourselves. Donny was the one who pointed it out."

"He has family, after all," Harley said with a small smile. "I'm glad. But I feel like you're only telling me bits and pieces. How does Dr. Douche… I mean Brooks, play into this?"

"The less you know, the better," Donny interjected, his tone brokering no argument. "But I don't like Catarina being alone with him right now."

"I'll send him in here," Harley offered, her tone shifting to one of resolve. "You're going to have to come up with a better excuse for your presence, though. He won't like a stranger being in a patient's room. Privacy issues and all."

"I'm not leaving," Donny said, his posture stiffening in defiance. "Catarina, it's time we called your brothers."

"Fine." The word came out as a sigh of resignation. My stomach churned with remorse and guilt, knowing what that call would set into motion. "But what are we going to tell Alex?"

"The truth," Donny replied with a sigh, his gaze turning serious. "I know he's a cop, but if we give him some of the truth, hiding what we need will be easier."

"Hiding what you need?" Harley echoed, blinking in confusion.

"Harley, there are things that have happened you don't need to worry about. But I will tell you, Dr. Brooks is not someone you should trust." I stepped toward her, lowering my voice. "He's involved with a man suspected of drug running and illegal dealings. I think…" I hesitated, choosing my words carefully. "I think he's supplying Fentanyl to Javier, the man I saw him with twice. Once in his office and once when I was on my date with Alex."

Donny's arm tightened around me possessively at the reminder, and Harley couldn't suppress a small laugh at his reaction, though she quickly sobered.

"Alex mentioned being here because of some big drug case he's working in Reno. Apparently, he was sent here as part of a joint task force to isolate the main supplier. He picked up John Doe's case, thinking it might be related. It's not," I said, the certainty in my voice surprising even me.

"How can you be sure?" Harley probed, her eyes narrowing in concern.

"Because the man lying behind me was kidnapped and tortured by another man in Vegas. His being here is merely coincidental. Donny's right. I need to call my brother. Michael Brighton is the man we've known as John Doe. He went missing months ago after my family became involved with a monster."

"A monster who is dead," Donny added, his tone flat and emotionless.

"What?" My eyes snapped to his, wide with shock. "He's dead?"

"Yes." Donny sighed, running a hand through his hair. "Matias Silva located him a month ago, shortly after you left. Vincenzo and Massimo flew to Chile. They'd hoped to get Michael's location, but

Dmitri knew telling them wouldn't change his fate. He is no longer a threat to you or your family, Catarina."

"Oh my God." The room seemed to spin, and I nearly collapsed, the weight of the news hitting me all at once. "My brother must be beside himself. And Mia?"

"Pregnant," Donny said, watching the flood of emotions cross my face as he shared the news.

"I'm going to let Dr. Brooks know he needs to come here to see you," Harley said, her voice softening as she took in my reaction. "I'll explain a family member has identified the patient, and you are with him."

"That's perfect, thanks," Donny replied with a nod, his voice calm and composed. Harley unlocked the door and stepped out, leaving us alone again.

"She's pregnant? I… I didn't know. I left without thinking about what I was leaving behind. My intentions were to have a normal life. I didn't mean to create more pain or death." I closed my eyes, finally allowing the tears I'd been holding back to fall.

"Stop." Donny's thumb brushed away the tears that streaked down my cheeks, his touch gentle despite the intensity of his words. "You aren't responsible for any of this, Cat. Michael is in that bed because of a sick man. The man you killed is dead because the doctor, who I suspect works with a drug lord, involved you in his shady dealings. Intentions, no matter how innocent, can turn deadly in the blink of an eye."

"But my family is still hurting, even after Dmitri's death. And all this time, I was blind to what was right in front of me because I didn't want to think about who I was. For weeks, Donny…weeks, Michael has been all alone in this hospital bed."

"He hasn't been alone, baby." Donny pulled me into his arms, his voice a quiet reassurance that I desperately needed. "He's had you."

A knock at the door startled me, and I stepped out of Donny's embrace, hastily wiping my tears away just as Dr. Brooks walked in.

"Miss Cook said I needed to come speak with you in here. Apparently, you've determined the patient's identity." Dr. Brooks looked suspiciously between Donny and me, his eyes narrowing as he assessed the situation. "And you are?"

A knock at the door had me quickly stepping out of Donny's embrace. I hastily wiped away the tears, trying to pull myself together just as Dr. Brooks walked in. His eyes immediately zeroed in on Donny, suspicion flickering across his face.

"Miss Cook said I needed to come speak with you in here. Apparently, you've determined the patient's identity," Dr. Brooks said, his tone cool and professional, though the undercurrent of distrust was hard to miss. "And you are?" He directed the question at Donny, his gaze narrowing.

"Dr. Brooks," I interjected, stepping between the two men, trying to defuse the tension. "This is Donny Russo. As crazy as this sounds, Donny is my fiancé and came to surprise me. We had a falling out when I moved here, but that's not important right now. What is important is the man lying behind me." I gestured toward Michael, taking a deep breath to steady myself before continuing. "A friend of the family went missing a few weeks before I moved here. We thought he had been in an accident while he was traveling." The lie felt natural, as if I'd rehearsed it a thousand times. "When Donny got here today and saw me in the room with him—" I pointed to Michael's still form. "He knew immediately who it was."

Dr. Brooks raised an eyebrow, clearly unconvinced. "A friend of the family? How is it you didn't recognize him yourself? You've been caring for him for weeks, Miss Aniston."

I saw Donny's jaw tighten at the mention of my fake name, a flicker of annoyance crossing his face. But I pressed on, determined to keep the story straight. "He wasn't recognizable under the bandages. Even when I changed them out, his face was too badly beaten. It wasn't until Donny made me really look at him that the familiarity hit me."

Dr. Brooks pursed his lips, clearly processing the information. "And the Detective? Has he confirmed his identity?"

"I haven't called him yet," I admitted, my voice steady. "I was about to do that when Nurse Cook informed me you were looking for me."

"Well, it appears this takes priority. What I needed can wait. Let me know what you find out," Dr. Brooks said curtly before turning on his heel and storming out of the room, leaving a trail of tension in his wake.

As soon as the door closed behind him, Donny let out a long breath, running his palm over his face in frustration. "I don't like him."

"That makes two of us," I replied, my voice laced with unease. "Let's go. We can use the breakroom to call Massimo. But Donny," I paused, my hand resting on the door handle as I gathered my thoughts. "Can we hold off on telling him about my issue? I want the focus to be on Michael for now. Once they get over that shock, we can tell them the rest."

Donny's expression softened slightly, though his protective stance didn't waver. "Fine, but I won't be leaving your side. Ever."

His words were more than just a promise of protection; they were a declaration of intent. He wasn't just promising to keep me safe—he was promising not to leave me again, to stay by my side no matter what. The realization hit me hard, causing a swirl of emotions to stir within me. If I told him I wanted to stay in this town, I had no doubt he would sacrifice everything, even his place beside my brother, to make that happen.

That thought made me question every decision I had made up until now. I had left my family, changed my name, and tried to build a new life, all in an attempt to find some semblance of normalcy. But now, with everything crashing down around me, I couldn't help but wonder if I was ready for what was coming next.

Because things were about to blow up in this tiny town, and there would be no going back.

thirteen

DONNY

I WATCHED as Catarina paced the tiny space, her every movement betraying the turmoil churning inside her. I knew making this call was hard on her for multiple reasons. She was going to have to face the decision she'd made to walk away from who she was. Her bloodline was more than just a family—it was a way of life. A life she clearly fought against being a part of no matter how deeply it was etched into her soul.

"You ready?" I asked, my phone lying on the cheap breakroom table like a ticking time bomb, waiting for the inevitable explosion.

"Yeah. Just do it," she whispered, pressing her palms against the table, and staring at the black screen as if it held all the answers she desperately needed.

I flicked the phone to life and pressed the button. The sound of ringing filled the room, each tone tightening the knot in my gut.

"Donny." Massimo's voice came through, steady and commanding as ever. "I was beginning to wonder if you remembered us."

"I have news." I didn't waste any time, knowing we couldn't afford to dance around the truth.

"You've found my sister?" His voice carried a hopeful edge that made Catarina suck in a sharp breath.

"He found me," she spoke, her voice trembling under the weight of her shame. I felt her pain as if it were my own.

"Catarina," Massimo whispered, his voice thick with emotion. "*Dio ti ha riportato a noi.*"

God has brought you back to us.

Over the years, I'd picked up enough Italian to understand what he'd said. The pain he felt had been my own since the day she'd called me for help.

"I'm so sorry, Massimo. I thought I knew what I wanted, but I didn't think leaving would cause so much hurt." Her tears splashed onto the shiny surface of the table. The sound was barely audible but cutting through me like a knife.

"Stop," Massimo snapped, his voice suddenly hard. "You don't owe me an apology. I understand why you did it. This life is not an easy one, and I've known since you could talk that you wanted something different. I just wish you'd told me, Cat. I could have helped you... could have made sure you were safe. Are you safe?" His voice cracked, revealing the depth of his concern.

Catarina shot me a knowing glance, her eyes pleading for reassurance.

"She's fine," I said, clearing my throat. "But there is something you need to know. Something the family needs to know."

"This sounds like the opposite of safe," Massimo growled, his tone shifting from concern to suspicion. "Where are you?"

"Lake District, Oregon."

"Oregon? What the fuck are you doing in Oregon?" He unleashed a string of Italian curses. "You left us to be free, but you only moved ten hours away." He let out a dry chuckle. "How did you find her, Donny?"

"That's a story for another day, *fratello*," I sighed, rubbing the back of my neck. "Catarina is a nurse here at the local hospital. She works in the Intensive Care Unit, specifically with patients needing long-term care."

"Okay. Are you needing me to dig up information on a patient? Do I need to get Alec on the call?"

"No, Massimo. When Catarina started working here, there was a patient who had been in the hospital for a few weeks. He was found dumped in the desert that borders the forest here in Oregon. Some local hikers found him and notified the authorities. This man has been unconscious the entire time and until recently, his face had been bandaged. Hell," I took a deep breath, steadying myself for what was coming next. "He's still unrecognizable to people who don't know him."

"Why haven't the authorities identified him yet?" Massimo's tone grew serious, the gravity of the situation starting to sink in.

"It wouldn't matter if they took DNA or fingerprints from him. People like us ensure we can't be identified." I paused, letting the significance of my words settle over him.

"People like us?" Massimo's voice dropped, growing quiet. "Donny, what aren't you saying?"

"Massimo," Catarina moved beside me, leaning closer to the phone as I pressed my palm against her back, trying to lend her strength. "You need to understand that if I had known when I got here, I would have called you sooner. I didn't know." A sob escaped her lips, the sound ripping through me.

"If you'd known what, Catarina? What the hell is going on, Donny?"

"The man I've been caring for isn't a stranger," she whimpered, her voice breaking as she struggled to get the words out. "Massimo, it's Michael. Michael is my patient."

Silence fell over the line, the kind that makes your heart stop. Then, without another word, Massimo spoke, his voice low and filled with resolve. "I'll be there tonight." The line went dead, leaving Catarina and me staring at the darkened screen in stunned silence.

Catarina crumpled against me, her cries of anguish tearing at the very fiber of my being. I wrapped my arms around her, pulling her close, trying to shield her from the storm raging inside her. Her pain was my pain, and I wanted more than anything to make it vanish, to take it all away. But this wasn't something I could fix. This was her demon, and she would need to be the one to exorcise it. All I could do was hold her and make sure she was safe.

"I know this isn't a good time, but we need to talk about the other issue," I murmured, my voice gentle but firm, reminding her of the other danger lurking in the shadows.

Catarina took a shaky breath, blowing it out slowly as she sat up in my lap, straightening her scrub top with trembling hands. "I need to go see Dr. Brooks."

"No." My fingers dug into her hips, holding her in place, unwilling to let her put herself at risk. "We talked about this."

"I'm in the hospital," she argued, trying to wiggle out of my grasp. "He won't do anything to jeopardize his career. It's the only way he'll open up about his friend." Catarina moved toward the door.

Her determination was clear in every step. "My shift is nearly over. Go back to Michael's room, and I will meet you there."

But I was faster, slamming the lock in place and pinning her between me and the door. "You're not making decisions about this, Catarina. I won't let you put yourself in danger. I can't."

Her palms pressed against my chest, trying to push me away, but I wasn't going to budge. Not when she was about to walk into the hornet's nest unprepared.

"Please," she whimpered, her body sagging against mine, the fight draining out of her.

I gripped her chin gently between my fingers, tilting her head up so she had to look me in the eyes. "No," I said softly but firmly. A lone tear trickled down her cheek, staining the cotton fabric of her shirt.

I leaned in slowly, giving her the chance to pull away. But when she didn't, I pressed my lips against hers. The kiss started softly, a promise of comfort and love, but it quickly grew heated, fueled by the desperation, and fear we both felt. Her hands wound around my neck, pulling me closer as I lifted her off the ground.

"Catarina," I growled against her lips as she ground her tiny frame against the bulge threatening to rip apart the metal teeth of my zipper.

"Make me forget," she whispered, her voice a breathy plea as she nibbled on my earlobe, rubbing herself against me.

With a quick spin, I took two long strides to the small love seat against the wall and sat down, pulling her onto my lap. Catarina straddled my legs, her lips continuing their exploration against my neck as I tugged her shirt over her head, tossing it to the floor.

"Last chance to back out," I warned, my fingertips trailing down her bare skin, savoring the feel of her beneath my hands.

Catarina responded by tugging my shirt from my pants and helping me out of it. She slipped off my legs and dropped to her knees between my legs. Her hands reached for the button of my jeans, and as though she had been an expert, she flicked open the button with ease. Her delicate palm slipped beneath the metal cage containing my arousal and wrapped her long fingers around my shaft. My body tensed, and I bucked my hips at the feel of her palm moving against my dick.

"Fuck." I hissed as she tugged my cock out of the confines of my jeans. She tugged at the material, silently asking me to lift my ass off the couch. When I did, she wiggled the fabric down to my ankles.

As soon as my pants hit the floor, Catarina had my dick shoved down her throat. Her hand cupped my testicles as she licked and sucked the swollen mushroom head, dripping with desire. Catarina moved with precision as she bobbed along my length. She was a goddess when it came to sucking cock, and if I let her continue, I would explode inside her sweet mouth. As good as I knew it would feel, I needed to be inside her.

"Stop." I tugged her to her feet. "Take off your scrubs."

I stroked my shaft, watching as she pushed her cotton pants down and stepped out of them. Holding my hand out, I guided her to my lap. She eagerly climbed onto the couch, straddling my hips once again. Her core hovered above my erection as she held my gaze. I held my shaft still and guided it between her folds as she sank down over me.

"Fuck." I groaned as she adjusted her gait to take me deeper. "You feel good."

Her breaths came out in pants as she began to move against me. Catarina pressed her palms to my shoulders, giving her something to hold on to as she fucked me. My hips thrust up, pressing into her as she rocked. We were like a symphony of sex, playing a song that thundered with desire. The muscles of my legs burned as I pounded into her, marking the depths of her womb as mine. Her head flew backward as her walls began to ripple around my rod. The pressure of her orgasm triggered my own. I bellowed into the room as my release ripped through me, filling her core with my seed. Catarina cried out as her pussy flooded with desire, coating my cock in her essence.

"Jesus Christ." I heaved out a breath. "Did I hurt you?" I ran my hand up her back, fisting her hair.

"No." She twisted her head in my palm and smiled. "Thank you."

"For what?"

"Aside from thoroughly fucking me?" Catarina smiled sheepishly as she eased off my lap and gathered her clothes. "For making me feel something other than guilt." She grabbed a wad of paper towels and wiped off the remnants of our coupling. Crumpled paper towels landed on my lap, making me laugh.

"Thanks… and you're welcome." I smiled. "Catarina, you can't confront your boss. Not yet. Let's get through the next day with your brothers first. Then we will come up with a plan."

She paused, seeming to mull over my words for a moment. "Okay."

"Okay?" Her compliance surprised me.

"Yes, okay. I don't think I can deal with anything else right now. Waiting a day won't hurt anything."

I stood and tugged my pants back into place. After slipping on my shirt, I moved to stand beside her. My finger traced her jaw, and I placed a kiss on her lips.

"I love you, Catarina."

"I love you, too."

CATARINA

SITTING BESIDE MICHAEL'S BED, the reality of what was happening slowly seeped into my bones, making everything feel surreal. It was as if I were floating outside my own body, watching the events unfold from a distance. After my shift ended the night before, Donny had taken me home, his presence a steady anchor in the storm of emotions I was battling. He'd put me to bed like I was something fragile, something he needed to protect. When I woke in the morning, wrapped in his arms, a sense of dread had settled over me, knowing today would be one of the hardest days I'd ever face. The warmth of his touch, the way he guided me into the shower and gently cared for me, was comforting, but it didn't ease the anxiety gnawing at my insides. Now, as I sat staring at Michael, Donny's hand laced in mine, I could feel my heart pounding in my chest, a steady drumbeat of fear and uncertainty.

The sound of voices rising in the hallway pulled me back to the present, my heart skipping a beat as I realized my family had arrived. A cold wave of anticipation washed over me, and I felt Donny's hand slip from mine as he stood, breaking the connection between us.

"Catarina." His voice was gentle, but I could hear the concern that laced every syllable.

"I know. They're here." I tried to steady my breathing, forcing myself to stand. My legs felt like they were made of lead, each step toward the door heavier than the last. "You ready?"

Donny nodded. His expression was unreadable as he moved the chairs out of the way. I paused, hand on the door, trying to brace myself for what was about to happen. When I finally opened it, the sight of my brothers' broad backs nearly took my breath away. All three of them were gathered around Harley, their voices overlapping in a chaotic blend of worry and frustration as they demanded to see Michael.

"It's okay, Harley. They're family," I said, my voice barely above a whisper, but it cut through the noise like a knife.

Massimo spun around at the sound of my voice, and before I could even blink, I was enveloped in their arms. The force of their embrace was overwhelming, a mixture of relief, love, and an undercurrent of hurt that I could feel in every touch. Tears welled up in my eyes and spilled over, blurring my vision as I clung to them, my body shaking with the weight of all the emotions I'd been holding back for so long. Their hands were on my back, in my hair, each touch grounding me, reminding me of what I'd left behind.

"Catarina." Vincenzo's voice was thick with emotion as he stepped back, his hands still resting on my shoulders, his eyes searching my face. "You're okay."

"Yes. I'm so sorry, Vincenzo." My voice broke as the tears kept coming, unstoppable now that the dam had burst.

"Stop." His voice was gentle but firm, his gaze steady. "You're here, and that's all that matters."

I turned to Antonio, and the sight of his red-rimmed eyes, filled with unshed tears, nearly shattered me. I stepped into his arms, holding him tightly as if he might disappear if I let go. The moment he broke down, his sobs racking his body, I felt my own heart break all over again. His pain was raw, visceral, and it cut through me like a blade.

"He's alive, Antonio." My words were shaky as I pulled back just enough to meet his gaze. "Michael's alive."

Antonio's eyes searched mine, hope battling with disbelief as he swiped at his tears. A shaky smile spread across his face as the realization began to sink in. "Where is he?"

"Come on. I'll take you to him." I took his hand, the connection between us feeling both fragile and unbreakable as I led him into the room where Michael lay. As soon as Antonio saw him, he froze, his breath catching in his throat. The sight of Michael—so fragile, so broken—seemed to paralyze him. I watched as Donny placed a reassuring hand on his back before quietly stepping into the hall, leaving us alone.

"What can you tell me?" Antonio's voice was a whisper, thick with emotion, as he took a hesitant step toward the bed.

"He was here before I came to Oregon. A group of hikers found his body and alerted the police. When he was brought into the ER, it was touch and go. He suffered crushed fingers—three missing from the left hand—both wrists were broken, and his right shoulder. On top of that, he had a punctured lung and a ruptured spleen. The damage to his face was extensive. Michael was tortured to the point of death. In fact, I think they left him for dead. He should be dead." My voice was clinical, detached, a coping mechanism I'd developed to keep the horror at bay. But inside, I was screaming. "The swelling on his brain took some time to go down, but he still hasn't woken up. The last CT showed normal brain activity, but his injuries were so severe, the doctor isn't sure what kind of long-term damage he'll have."

Antonio's hand trembled as he gently lifted Michael's bandaged hand, pressing a kiss over the gauze. The sight of my brother, usually so strong, so unshakable, brought to his knees by the sight of the man he loved, was almost too much to bear.

"I didn't believe Massimo when he told me you'd been found and that you were with Michael. Mia and I prayed we'd find closure regarding his disappearance, but the longer we waited, the more we accepted he was likely dead. This is a miracle." Antonio's voice cracked as he leaned down, resting his forehead on the bed beside Michael's still form. "I don't care if he's got problems. I love him, and nothing will change that."

"And Mia?" I asked softly, stepping closer and resting a hand on his back, feeling the tremors that still ran through him.

"She wanted to come, but I needed to be sure. If it hadn't been him, I was worried about how she would react. She's pregnant, you know." Antonio's voice was filled with a quiet awe, as if he still couldn't quite believe it. "It's his—the baby. We found out not long after the twins were born. Mia and I cried when the doctor told us. Even though we thought we lost him, we still had a piece of him to hold on to. And now…"

"Now you have him, too," I whispered, my throat tight with emotion as I rubbed my brother's back, offering what little comfort I could.

"I'm going to step outside and give you some time alone with him," I added, my voice barely holding steady as I pulled away. The weight of the moment was almost suffocating, but I knew Antonio needed this time with Michael more than anything.

"Thank you, Catarina. I was so mad at you for leaving like you did, but if you hadn't, we wouldn't have him back. I think it was supposed to happen this way."

His words lingered in the air as I slipped from the room, closing the door softly behind me. The reality of Michael's condition settled heavily on my shoulders. He was alive, but his recovery would be long and arduous. The physical damage was severe, but the emotional and psychological scars would be even harder to heal. We didn't know what kind of life he would wake up to, or if he would even recognize the world around him when he did.

"Catarina." Vincenzo's voice brought me back to the present, his concern palpable as he approached. "How is he?"

"Michael or Antonio?" I asked, leaning against the wall, the exhaustion beginning to seep into my bones.

"Both," Vincenzo replied, glancing toward the closed door with a mixture of hope and worry.

"They're together. That's all that matters right now. The rest will work itself out," I said, though my voice lacked conviction. The truth was, I wasn't sure if everything would work out. But I knew I had to hold on to that hope for my brothers, for all of us. "I'm sorry for leaving the way I did. I should have talked to you guys and told you what I wanted. You must hate me for missing out on my niece and nephew's birth."

Vincenzo pulled me into a hug, his arms strong and steady around me. "I could never hate you," he said softly, his voice filled with warmth. "Pissed, maybe. But hate? That's not a word in my vocabulary for you, Cat."

"So…" He stepped back, looking around the hospital hallway with an expression that was both curious and resigned. "This is home for you?"

I hesitated, the weight of his question pressing down on me like a lead blanket. "I thought it was," I admitted, my voice tinged with regret. "But seeing you guys here, I know it was just an escape."

"Does that mean you'll come home with us?" Massimo asked, his voice hopeful but cautious, as if he was afraid to push too hard.

"Not right away. I owe it to the hospital to work out a notice. But this isn't home for me. Not anymore." My eyes found Donny's across the hallway, and a blush crept up my neck as I saw the understanding in his gaze, the silent promise that he would be with me no matter where I chose to go.

"I get it. You're coming home for a man," Massimo teased, quirking an eyebrow with a knowing smirk. "I can't say I'm sad about that. You've kept my best friend away too long. Madison is going nuts with Drew as my second. He gets on her nerves. Truth is, I think he's smitten with my fiancée, and is just as protective as I am."

"And you haven't killed him?" I managed to laugh, the sound a welcome relief from the tension that had been building.

"Nah. Drew is harmless. He likes his balls intact," Massimo said with a grin, and I couldn't help but laugh again, the sound feeling strange but good.

"Trina." Harley's voice cut through our conversation, and I turned to see her approaching, her expression tinged with worry.

The use of my fake name made Massimo narrow his eyes at me, suspicion flickering in his gaze. "Trina?"

"Yeah." Harley leaned in, whispering so only we could hear. "I figured she didn't want Dr. Brooks hearing her real name."

"Catarina," Massimo growled, his gaze pinning me with a mixture of concern and frustration. "Is there something you left out?"

I felt my chest tighten, the weight of everything I hadn't told him pressing down on me like a vice. "She used a fake name to get hired. If her boss finds out, she could face legal troubles," Donny interjected, his voice calm but firm, offering me a lifeline in a situation that was rapidly spiraling out of control. "Harley knows but has no intention of spilling the beans."

"I see." Massimo's shoulders relaxed slightly, though I could tell he wasn't completely satisfied with the explanation. "Is that all?" His gaze remained sharp, searching for any sign that there was more I wasn't telling him.

"Excuse me." A new voice cut through the tension, and my heart sank as I turned to see Alex stepping out of the elevator.

"Detective Coulter." I forced a smile, the sight of him sending a wave of guilt crashing over me. I stepped around my brothers to meet him at the counter, my mind racing as I tried to figure out what to say.

"Holy fuck." Alex's eyes widened as he took in the sight of Massimo. "Massimo?"

"Alex Coulter, it's been a long time." Massimo's voice was warm as he extended his hand, but there was a tension in the air that made my stomach churn.

"Um." My head whipped back and forth between them, confusion swirling in my mind. "You two know each other?"

"You could say that." Massimo's grin was sharp, but there was something dangerous in his eyes. "Alex and I went to college together. But I thought you lived in Reno, a cop out there."

"I was… I mean, I am. I'm on special assignment as part of a joint drug task force. Lake District might be small, but it's the perfect hiding spot for drug trafficking."

Massimo bristled at his words, his gaze cutting to me with a look that sent a shiver down my spine. I ducked my head, unable to meet his eyes, knowing that if I did, he would see everything I was trying to hide. He still didn't know how Donny had found me, and when he learned the truth, the small town of Lake District would learn the Anastasi name in a way that I wasn't ready for.

"I see. Well, it looks like you've met my sister," Massimo said, the words heavy with implication.

Alex's head snapped toward me, his eyes narrowing with a mixture of disbelief and anger. "Your sister?"

"Yeah. Catarina. She came here to get away from the family. As it turns out, she's been caring for a family member who went missing. Michael was listed as John Doe—that's why we couldn't find him after his accident."

"Accident," Alex muttered, the disbelief clear in his tone. "The man in that room is family?" His eyes were locked on mine, demanding answers I wasn't ready to give.

"Yes." Massimo's voice was calm, but I could see the tension simmering beneath the surface. "Am I missing something here?"

"It seems your sister has some explaining to do. Isn't that right, Trina? Or should I call you Catarina?" Alex's voice was cold, each word a sharp edge that cut into me.

"Alex." I stepped forward, desperation clawing at my throat, but Donny's arm wrapped around my middle, holding me back, grounding me. "I only lied about my name. Everything else was real."

"Right." Alex's voice was dripping with sarcasm, and the disappointment in his eyes cut through me like a knife. "I guess I can mark John Doe out of my investigation. Harley—" he turned to my friend with a tight smile. "Call me if you need anything." He turned back to us, his gaze hardening as he addressed Massimo. "Massimo, it was nice seeing you again. I hope Michael makes a full recovery. Catarina."

"Alex. Please. Don't go like this." My voice broke, the guilt and regret crashing over me in waves, but I could see in his eyes that it was too late.

"Look." He glanced around at my brothers, his gaze lingering on Donny for a moment before he continued. "You and I were never going to happen—not when he showed up, and probably not before. And I'm good with that, really, I am. But I don't like liars. You could have told me who you were and why you'd chosen to change your name. People do it all the time for different reasons, but you didn't and had me believing you were genuine. I overlook a lot of things as a cop. But..." He glanced at Massimo, something unspoken passing between them, something that made my heart twist with fear. "As silly as it sounds, I don't tolerate liars."

"Hey." Massimo stepped forward, his voice a mix of authority and concern. "Don't hold it against her, Alex. She was trying to protect you, too. You know my family. It was the right thing to do."

"Sure." Alex's voice was cold, the walls between us now impenetrable. "I've got to go. But Catarina... you should stay away from Javier. He's bad news."

With that, he turned and walked toward the elevator, leaving me standing there, feeling as if the floor had just dropped out from under me.

"Who's Javier?" Vincenzo's voice broke through the suffocating silence, the question hanging heavy in the air.

"Trina?" Dr. Brooks's voice sliced through the tension, his tone sharp as he stepped out of the shadows. "Meet me in my office. Now."

"Fuck," Donny muttered under his breath, his frustration barely contained.

"I'll be fine," I whispered, forcing a smile as I pressed a kiss to his cheek, trying to reassure him—and myself. But as I followed my boss down the hallway, the weight of everything that had just happened pressed down on me like a vice, squeezing the air from my lungs. There was no telling how much Dr. Brooks had overheard, and I knew that whatever it was, it was enough to make my already precarious situation even worse. The last thing I needed was him knowing who my family was, because once he did, I had no doubt that he would use that knowledge to his advantage. And as I walked down that hallway, I couldn't shake the feeling that my problems were about to go from bad to catastrophic.

CATARINA

MY EYES TRACKED Catarina as she walked down the corridor, every step taking her further away from me. The tightness in my chest grew with each passing second until she disappeared from view, leaving me alone with a hollow ache that settled deep in my gut. Massimo and Vincenzo were glaring at me, their eyes burning into the side of my head like twin daggers. I could feel their anger simmering, the need for answers boiling just beneath the surface.

"Talk. Now," Massimo growled, his voice low and dangerous as soon as I turned to face them.

"Not here. Let's step inside Michael's room," I suggested, trying to keep my tone steady as I ushered them inside. The air in the room felt heavy, oppressive even, as I closed the door behind us. Antonio was on FaceTime with Mia, filling her in on Michael's condition. Her tears were both heartbreaking and joyful, the conflicting emotions palpable even through the screen.

"Hey, Rach, baby. I need to call you back," Antonio said softly, his eyes flicking to Massimo's stiff posture. He promised to call her later before ending the call and slipping his phone into his pocket. "What's up?" he asked, his voice tight with worry.

"Catarina's in trouble," I said, not sugarcoating the situation. There was no time for that. "You asked how I found her. The truth is, she found me. Three nights ago, I got a call from her. It was a burner phone, but I'd suspected for some time that she'd been calling me and not saying anything… until this time. She said she was in trouble and needed me. After getting her location, I drove here."

"Okay. What's going on?" Vin's pacing had an edge of desperation to it, a man trying to make sense of something he couldn't control.

"When I got here, she was sitting on the floor of her kitchen covered in blood. A man had been dead for several hours at her feet." The memory was still too fresh, the image of her broken and trembling burned into my mind. "Apparently, Catarina fought the intruder off and stabbed him. Your friend Alex had just dropped her off from a date. As soon as she stepped inside, the man attacked her. Catarina said he was there to take her for his boss. Javier Costa."

"Fuck," Massimo groaned, rubbing his temples as if he could ward off the headache forming there. "How did she get tangled up with someone capable of kidnapping her?"

"Her boss." The words came out like poison, my teeth grinding together in frustration. "She overheard a conversation between him and Javier a day or so before her date with Alex. Catarina believes Dr. Brooks is supplying him with drugs or helping him transport them."

"Fucking Christ," Antonio groaned, his hand raking through his hair in frustration. "Why can't we catch a break?"

"The good news is she's agreed to come home. Maybe we can just pack her up and leave without incident," I suggested, though I knew the likelihood of that was slim. Nothing in our world was ever that simple.

"You know as well as I do, people like Javier will not let her leave if he suspects she knows something," Massimo said, his voice laced with the grim reality of our situation.

He was right, of course. In our world, criminals didn't leave loose ends, and to Javier Costa, Catarina was a loose end that needed tying up. The thought of her being in his crosshairs made my blood run cold.

"Let me call Drew. He's at the hotel and can help us get some information on the motherfucker. Even if I thought he would let her just leave, he fucked up when he threatened her life." Massimo's voice was tight with controlled rage as he stepped into the hallway, already pulling out his phone.

"We need to make arrangements for Michael's transfer. I want him in Vegas, where I can oversee his recovery," Antonio said, his gaze never leaving Michael's battered form on the bed.

"Go do that. Vincenzo and I will go talk to Harley and see what she can tell us about the lovely Dr. Brooks. When Catarina is done meeting with the prick, we'll head over to her house and come up with a plan," I said, my mind already running through the logistics of what needed to happen.

Antonio nodded, joining Massimo in the corridor, leaving me alone with Vincenzo. He blew out a frustrated breath, his eyes lingering on Michael with a mixture of relief and guilt.

"I prayed my brother would get closure, but not at the expense of my sister's life," he said quietly, the weight of those words hanging in the air between us.

"I will protect her with every breath in my body," I promised, my voice hardening as I met his gaze. "You really love her, don't you?" Vincenzo asked, his tone softening, the anger replaced with something deeper, more profound.

"With all that I am. I let her slip through my fingers once, but I won't do it again. If I have to bind and gag her, she'll be coming home with me to Vegas. And then I'm marrying her."

"All right then." Vincenzo's lips twitched into a small smile, the tension between us easing just a fraction. "Let's go learn about the doctor."

I followed him out of the room, my mind a whirlwind of plans and possibilities. Harley was seated behind the nurse's station, filling out some paperwork. She jumped slightly when I approached, her eyes widening in surprise.

"Harley," I said softly, not wanting to startle her again. "Sorry. Didn't mean to make you jump. I wondered if we could ask you some questions about your boss."

"Dr. Douche?" She pursed her lips, her dislike for the man evident in every syllable. "Sorry. I don't like him. Sure, you can ask me anything."

We spent the next thirty minutes learning everything we could about Dr. Brooks, piecing together the puzzle that had led to this moment. Harley had been at the hospital for three years and knew the man well enough to paint a clear picture. She told us about his nasty divorce, how his ex-wife had cleaned him out financially, leaving him desperate and vulnerable. It didn't take much to connect the dots—Dr. Brooks had gotten tangled up with Javier Costa because of money. Desperate people made bad choices, and those choices had deadly consequences.

"You thinking what I'm thinking?" Vincenzo asked, a dark grin spreading across his face. "This doctor's in bed with some bad dude over money."

"Yep. And he fucked up, threatening Catarina," I replied, the anger simmering just beneath the surface.

"Yes, he did." There was a wicked glint in Vincenzo's eyes, one that sent a shiver down my spine. "I feel sorry for him."

"You do?" I asked, tilting my head in confusion.

"He had no idea the monster he works with is nothing compared to the monster I am. He signed his death certificate the moment he took part in sending that goon to hurt her."

"You're one scary motherfucker, Vin. I'm glad you consider me family," I said with a chuckle, though there was a seriousness to my words.

"It was only a matter of time before you became family for real. We all knew you were in love with our sister—at least we suspected it. Massimo couldn't be happier that his best friend will be the man to guard our sister in all the ways that matter."

"I'd die for her, but not before making him bleed out—that I can promise you," I said, the conviction in my voice leaving no room for doubt.

"Well, how about you don't do that. Let's just clean this mess up and bring my baby sister home," Vincenzo suggested, his tone light but the intent behind it deadly serious.

"Deal." I smiled, though my mind was already racing with the details of our next steps. "You might have to help me tie her up and drag her back."

Vincenzo laughed, the sound a rare moment of levity in an otherwise dark day. "Good thing I know a bit about using ropes." He winked, the mischievous glint in his eyes a stark contrast to the grim reality we were facing.

"I don't think your sister needs to know about your sexual preferences. Besides, if anyone is going to introduce her to being tied up, it'll be me," I shot back, though the thought of Catarina in that situation sent a thrill of protectiveness—and something darker—through me.

"How about you keep that shit to a minimum? You might be like family to me, but I'll cut your dick off in a second if I have to think about where you put it," Vincenzo replied, his voice tinged with both humor and a deadly seriousness.

"Deal." I nodded, knowing there were lines even *we* wouldn't cross.

We headed back into Michael's room, the tension in the air thickening as we waited for Catarina to return. She wasn't going to like our plan, but it was for her safety. And while I'd been joking with Vincenzo, I wasn't above tying her up and forcing her back to Vegas. Whatever it took to keep her safe, I would do it. No matter the cost.

sixteen

CATARINA

THE MOMENT I stepped into his office. A cold dread settled over me like a lead weight. The air felt thick, suffocating, and my pulse quickened as my eyes adjusted to the dim light. There, in the shadowed corner, sat Javier Costa, his leg casually crossed over his knee as if he owned the place. The sight of him sent a jolt of fear straight through me, but I forced myself to remain calm. Dr. Brooks, with a twisted smile, shut the office door with a deliberate click, engaging the lock. My stomach churned, a sickening mix of fear and anger rising as I realized just how much trouble I was in.

"Catarina," Dr. Brooks sneered, his voice dripping with condescension as he perched himself on the edge of his desk. He pulled out a chair, gesturing for me to sit. The casual way he tried to assert control over me made my skin crawl. "I see you've lied about your name on your employment paperwork. Whatever should I do with that information?" His eyes flicked toward Javier, his smile widening with sinister glee. "What do you think, Javier? Should we report her?"

The way they played off each other, like predators toying with their prey, sent a shiver down my spine. Javier leaned forward, uncrossing his leg, and planting his foot firmly on the floor. His eyes bore into me, cold and calculating. "I think we could find something more useful than getting her in trouble." He let the words hang in the air for a moment, letting them seep into my consciousness. "Tell me, Miss Anastasi. How much would your brothers pay to have you returned in one piece?"

My breath hitched, panic clawing at my chest. I knew I had to get out of there. I pushed against the chair, trying to stand, but Dr. Brooks was quicker. He shoved me back down with a force that left me stunned.

"Not so fast." His voice was a cruel taunt, his grip on my shoulder firm and unyielding.

"You're crazy," I spat out, trying to mask the rising fear with bravado. "Threatening me with my family right outside the door."

"They let you come back here," he countered, his voice laced with arrogance. "Obviously, they don't believe I'm a threat, or one of them would have followed you in here."

A cold sweat broke out across my skin as the reality of my situation became painfully clear. I was alone in a room with two men who had every intention of harming me, and the people who could protect me were just a few doors away, completely unaware. My heart pounded relentlessly, the fear spreading like poison through my veins. "What are you going to do with me?" I asked, my voice trembling despite my best efforts to keep it steady.

"There is more than one way out of this hospital, Catarina. Surely, you're not that daft." His condescending tone made my stomach churn.

Javier stood and extended his hand toward Dr. Brooks, who reached into his desk drawer and pulled out something that made my blood run cold. A syringe. My eyes widened in horror as I realized what they intended to do.

"Hold up. You don't need to do something rash," I pleaded, my hands coming up in a defensive gesture as I instinctively leaned back, trying to distance myself from the threat.

Javier moved with a predator's grace, coming to my side in an instant. His presence loomed over me, suffocating, and when he grabbed my arm, I felt the sharp prick of the needle before I could react. The sting was followed by a burning sensation that spread quickly through my arm and into my bloodstream, making my head swim. The room started to tilt, my vision blurring as the sedative took hold. I tried to fight it, to stay alert, but my limbs felt heavy, uncooperative. I stumbled back into the chair, my body no longer obeying my commands.

Javier's grip on my upper arm tightened, pulling me against him with a force that made my ribs ache. The blunt end of a gun pressed into my side, a silent threat that left no room for defiance. "Now," he hissed, his voice low and menacing. "We're going to walk out of here, and you're not going to make a scene. You got it?"

My head bobbed weakly, the sedative making it nearly impossible to focus. My thoughts were muddled, slipping through my fingers like sand as I struggled to stay conscious. Javier opened the door, and the harsh fluorescent light of the hallway made me squint. Dr. Brooks stepped out first, his movements casual, as if this were just another day at the office.

As Javier pulled me along behind him, my eyes connected with Harley's across the hallway. The shock on her face was immediate, her mouth dropping open as she processed the scene unfolding before her. I saw the moment she decided to act, her body turning as if to call out, to get help. But she never had the chance.

Javier's gun came down with brutal efficiency, striking her head with a sickening thud. The sound echoed in the hallway, a hollow, final note that made my stomach lurch. I whimpered as Harley crumpled to the floor, her body limp and lifeless. Blood pooled beneath her head, spreading across the linoleum in a dark, crimson stain.

"Harley," I slurred, my voice barely more than a whisper as I tried to reach for her, tried to go to my friend. But Javier's grip was unyielding, his hand a vise around my arm as he yanked me down the hallway toward the rear stairwell. My heart broke at the sight of her lying there, and guilt washed over me in waves, making me nauseous. This was my fault. I had brought this danger into her life, and now she was paying the price.

Dr. Brooks pushed open the door to the stairwell, holding it open as Javier dragged me through. The cool air of the stairwell hit my face, but it did nothing to clear the fog in my mind. I was losing the battle to stay awake, the drug pulling me deeper into unconsciousness with every step. By the time we burst through the exterior door and into the blinding sunlight, I was barely aware of my surroundings.

The last thing I saw was the trunk of a car looming in front of me, dark and ominous. Then, as the lid closed over me, the world went black, swallowing me whole.

seventeen

DONNY

"IT'S TAKING her an awful long time with Dr. Brooks," Vincenzo muttered, glancing at his watch. His brow furrowed with concern. "Where'd that nurse go? Maybe she can check on Catarina without raising suspicion." He stepped into the doorway, his eyes scanning the hallway with an intensity that immediately put me on edge. "Something's wrong."

His words were like a jolt of electricity, spurring me into action. I pushed past him, my heart rate spiking as I entered the hallway.

"Why'd you say that?" I demanded, though a gnawing sense of dread was already taking root in my gut.

"Where's the other woman? Shouldn't she be coming by to check on patients? It's been over thirty minutes." Massimo joined us, his expression darkening as he questioned Harley's whereabouts. "Vin's right. Something is off."

Antonio, who had been standing vigil by Michael's side, moved toward us, but Massimo stopped him with a firm hand on his shoulder.

"No. You stay with him. Vin," he said, nodding toward me, "you and Donny go check down the hallway. That's the direction Dr. Brooks and Catarina went. I'm calling Drew. I want him here in case we need to beat the shit out of someone."

The urgency in his voice fueled my movements, and Vincenzo and I quickly made our way down the hallway. Each step felt like I was moving through quicksand, the mounting anxiety slowing time to a crawl. When we reached Dr. Brooks's office, the sight that greeted us made my blood run cold.

Harley lay sprawled on the floor, unconscious and bleeding. The crimson stain seeping from her head onto the sterile tiles was a sharp contrast against the stark white, and the metallic scent of blood filled my nostrils, twisting my stomach into knots.

"She's alive," Vincenzo said, his voice tight as he knelt to check her pulse. Relief briefly flickered through me, but it was overshadowed by the icy grip of fear. He quickly assessed her injuries, then lifted her into his arms with surprising gentleness. "Search his office. I'm taking her down to Michael's room. We need to keep this quiet. We don't need the police involved."

Nodding, I stepped into the office, my mind racing. The room was eerily tidy, as if nothing had happened, but my eyes were drawn to a syringe discarded on the floor. I crouched down, staring at it as a wave of rage and helplessness crashed over me. They had drugged her. Catarina wouldn't have gone willingly—she was too strong, too determined. But Javier had planned for that. He had known she would fight, and he had taken steps to ensure her compliance.

I rifled through the doctor's drawers, searching for anything that could give me a clue about where they had taken her. But the room yielded nothing, and the frustration gnawed at me, making my movements more frantic. Every second that passed felt like an eternity, each heartbeat hammering home the fact that Catarina was in danger, and I had no idea where she was.

I rushed back to Michael's room, where Vincenzo had already laid Harley on a gurney. He was on the phone, his expression grim as he relayed what little information we had. When he saw me, I shook my head, the despair in my eyes telling him I'd found nothing.

"He drugged her to get out of here," I muttered, moving to stand beside Harley. The sight of her lying there, so still, and vulnerable, made my chest tighten with a mix of anger and fear.

Massimo pushed through the door, Drew close on his heels. The tension in the room ratcheted up another notch as they joined us.

"Drew," I greeted him, though my voice was strained. "Glad you're here."

Drew's eyes flicked past me and locked onto Harley. The change in him was immediate and startling. He stepped closer, his usually composed demeanor cracking as he took in her injuries. "What the fuck happened? Where's Catarina?" Drew's voice was sharp, almost frantic, as he ran a hand down Harley's head, careful to avoid the wound on her temple. "Get me some fucking gauze. This needs to be cleaned and dressed."

I blinked in surprise at the venom in his voice, at the fierce protectiveness he was displaying toward a woman he didn't even know. In all the years I'd known Drew, I'd never seen him like this—so raw, so on edge.

"That's Catarina's supervisor and friend," I explained, my tone softening slightly as I tried to make sense of his reaction. "My guess is she stumbled upon them kidnapping Catarina."

"Motherfucker," Drew spat, taking the antiseptic Vincenzo handed him and tending to Harley's injuries with a tenderness that belied the anger simmering beneath the surface.

"You all right, Drew?" Massimo asked, his eyes narrowing as he observed Drew's uncharacteristic behavior.

"Yeah," Drew muttered, though his voice was tight with barely suppressed emotion. "This woman didn't deserve this. It just pisses me off."

"All right." Massimo didn't push further, but the confusion lingered in the air. "We need to find out whatever we can about this doctor. Vin, I want you and Drew to go to his house and see what you can find. Thanks to Harley, we have that info."

Drew hesitated, his eyes flicking back to Harley, concern etched into every line of his face. "You sure I'm not needed here?"

Massimo raised an eyebrow, clearly puzzled by Drew's reluctance to leave. "Positive."

"Right." Drew stepped back, his expression hardening as he turned to Vincenzo. "Let's go. Watch her. Make sure she doesn't throw up and choke."

"I'll make sure she's good," Antonio said, tipping his head toward the two men as they headed into the hallway.

"That was weird," I remarked, shaking my head in disbelief. Drew's reaction to Harley was something I hadn't anticipated, and it left me with more questions than answers.

"Madison will be here in two hours, Antonio," Massimo informed him, shifting gears. "She's going to ride back with the private medics I hired to transport Michael to your house. A doctor will be waiting to review his files, which I've already procured from Harley. I'll leave it up to you on whether you stay behind."

"Fuck." Antonio's voice cracked as he cradled his head in his hands, his elbows resting on his knees. "I don't know what to do. Catarina is my sister, but we've just found him."

"Go with Michael," I urged. The choice was clear to me, even if it was tearing Antonio apart. "We will bring Catarina home. He needs you more than she does."

"If something happens to her, I'd never forgive myself," Antonio whispered, his voice filled with a raw pain that resonated deep within me.

"I promise you I will do everything in my power to make sure she's safe," I said, the conviction in my words leaving no room for doubt. My only priority was Catarina. No one else mattered—not even my own life.

"Can someone tell me what the fuck is going on?" Alex's angry voice cut through the tension, drawing all eyes to him as he entered the room.

"Shit." Antonio glanced toward Massimo, a silent question in his eyes.

"Alex." Massimo sighed. His frustration was evident as he gestured for Alex to shut the door. "Shut the door."

Alex joined us, his presence adding another layer of urgency to the situation. "Why in the fuck is the nursing supervisor laying on a gurney with a bandage on her head?"

"It seems Dr. Brooks is in bed with Javier Costa," Massimo explained, his tone clipped.

"No shit," Alex grumbled. "I just received word from my superiors in Reno that his name came up in an online search as being connected to him through a dummy business."

"Well, he has Catarina," Massimo said, nodding toward Harley. "She was the unlucky victim of poor timing."

"I need to call this in." Alex reached for his phone, but before he could dial, I stepped forward and snatched it from his hand.

"You can't do that," I said, my voice low but firm.

"What the fuck do you mean, I can't do that?" Alex squared up to me, his posture tense, ready for a fight.

"Hey, calm down," Massimo intervened, pulling me back before things could escalate further. "Alex, I know you want to do the right thing, but we can't involve the cops."

"I am the cops," Alex shot back, crossing his arms over his chest, clearly not backing down.

"You know who I am, Alex. You have to understand why bringing in anyone else in a city we don't know could be detrimental to my family," Massimo said, his tone softening as he tried to reason with him.

Alex's eyes narrowed as he considered Massimo's words. "Explain."

Massimo and Antonio exchanged a glance, their silent communication speaking volumes. "We've just made it out from under the Feds' watch. Involving the police here would likely put us on their radar again. Vincenzo's wife just had their twins, and he nearly died. Not to mention Antonio." He nodded toward Antonio, who was watching the exchange with a haunted expression. "Please, Alex."

"This could cost me my job," Alex sighed, the weight of the decision pressing down on him.

"If that happens, come to Vegas. I could use a man like you," Massimo offered, though the words carried more gravity than just a job offer.

"You want me to work for the mob?" Alex furrowed his brows, clearly conflicted. "That's the opposite of what my job stands for, Massimo."

"Not really. You have this idea that we're bad guys who steal and murder. While I won't lie and say that's not a small fraction of the business, that's not all we are," Massimo countered, his voice calm and measured.

"Fine." Alex began pacing, his agitation evident. "But we need to do this as clean as possible. I don't want blood on my hands."

"Trust me. The blood won't be on yours," I growled, my mind already running through what needed to be done. "We need everything you have on Dr. Brooks and Javier Costa."

Alex shoved his hands into his pockets, his expression hardening as he huffed in frustration. Without another word, he walked out of the room, disappearing into the hallway.

"Should I go after him?" I asked, looking to Massimo for direction.

"No, he'll be back," Massimo replied, though his frown deepened as he pulled out his phone. The tension in the room was thick, everyone on edge.

"What is it?" Antonio asked, his voice strained as he stood from his chair.

"The twins have arrived in Vegas," Massimo said, his tone flat as he delivered the news.

"Wait." Antonio's hands flew to his head, fingers threading through his hair in disbelief. "You mean Carmela and Celestina are here in the States?"

"Yep." Massimo closed his eyes, leaning his head back against the wall. "They couldn't have picked worse timing."

"Shit." Antonio pressed his phone to his ear, his voice tinged with desperation as he explained the situation to Mia. The timing of the twins' arrival was a complication we hadn't anticipated, and it added another layer of stress to an already volatile situation.

"What the hell is going on?" Harley's voice, tinged with anger and confusion, cut through the tension as she slowly sat up on the gurney, her eyes darting around the room.

"Hey, take it easy," Massimo said, moving quickly to her side. "What do you remember?"

Harley rubbed her head, her face scrunching up in pain. "I was heading down to Dr. Brooks's office to check on Catarina…when— Oh my God, Catarina…" Panic surged through her voice as she tried to get off the gurney, but Massimo gently pushed her back down.

"Harley, you took a knock to the head and have been out for almost two hours. Don't try to get up just yet," he urged, his tone gentle but firm.

"But… they took her," Harley cried, her body trembling as sobs racked her frame. The sight of her falling apart hit me like a punch to the gut.

"Jesus Christ," Drew muttered, pushing past me to pull Harley into his arms. The possessiveness in his actions stunned me, but what shocked me more was how Harley clung to him, as if he was the only thing keeping her anchored to reality. Drew's voice was soft as he whispered something in her ear, rubbing her back in soothing circles.

Vincenzo stepped into the room, his presence making the already cramped space feel even smaller. "They've gone to Reno," he announced, his voice a grim statement of fact. "Evidence Drew and I recovered from the doc's house made it pretty clear they were going back to Javier's stomping grounds."

"He's right," Alex said, reappearing in the doorway. "I just got off the phone with my contact in Reno. He heard Javier is due back with something that will bring them a big payout."

"Catarina," I muttered, the name a bitter taste on my tongue. Every second she was in Javier's hands was a second too long.

"Yep," Massimo grunted, the tension in his body radiating out like a coiled spring ready to snap. "He thinks he can use Catarina as leverage to get something from me."

"Looks like we're going back to Reno," Alex said, his voice resigned but determined.

"I know you don't want to be part of this, Alex, and I respect that," Massimo said, his voice measured. "But if you could help us get situated in Reno, I'd appreciate it. That motherfucker has my sister, and I'm going to bring hellfire down on him and his entire operation."

"What about Harley?" Drew's voice was tight as he looked between us, the concern for her clear in his eyes.

"She'll go back with Antonio. It's safer in Vegas, and she's familiar with Michael's case," Massimo decided.

"Do I get a say?" Harley's voice cut through the tension, her eyes blazing with determination.

"No," Drew snapped, shooting her a look that brooked no argument. "You're not safe here."

"But this is my home. You can't just make me leave," she protested, her voice rising in frustration.

"Is your family here?" Drew asked, his tone softer but still firm.

"No." Her chin jutted out in defiance, but the vulnerability in her eyes gave her away.

"Harley," I interjected, stepping forward. "I know this is inconvenient, but you aren't safe here alone, and we can't stay. You would also be doing us a favor if you traveled with Antonio and Michael back to Vegas. Aside from Catarina and Dr. Brooks, you're the only one who knows his condition… and Catarina trusts you."

Harley's eyes flicked between us, weighing her options. Finally, she nodded, the fight leaving her. "Fine. But only for a few days. I need to make a phone call to my supervisor. They're going to need to cover my and Catarina's shifts."

"I'll take care of it," Massimo said, already moving toward the door before Harley could argue.

"Thank you," Antonio said, his relief palpable as he nodded toward her. But as I watched him, the weight of the situation bore down on me. We had to get Catarina back. No matter the cost, no matter what it took, I wouldn't rest until she was safe in my arms again.

eighteen

CATARINA

IT TOOK me a few seconds to get my bearings and realize I was in a trunk—still. I was surprised to find my hands and feet weren't bound. They must have thought the sedative would last the entire ride to wherever they were taking me. My eyes adjusted to the inside, allowing me to make out a few shapes inside the space housing me. The only light I had was the red illumination coming from the back taillights. It was closing in on nightfall, which indicated I'd been transported a good distance from Lake District. If I had to bet… we were going to Reno.

I rolled to my belly and tried to peer out the gap between the trunk and the plastic casing of the light. I couldn't see much, only that I was right, and it was dark. My palms skimmed the interior of the trunk, searching for something I could use as a tool. My body tensed when my fingers brushed across a small screwdriver. It was lodged between the floor and the car's edge, but using my nails, I pried it free.

My body lurched sideways and slammed into the backseat when the car came to a stop. I rolled back to my side and tucked the screwdriver into the waist of my scrubs, using the ties to hold it in place. I wanted them to believe I was still unconscious, so I lay as still as I could, waiting for the trunk to open.

The metal lid flew up, and hands wrapped around my shoulders. My body was wrenched up and tossed onto the pavement, making me cry out in pain. I immediately covered my face, anticipating a hit.

"Get up." Dr. Brooks kicked me in the side, causing the air to whoosh out of my lungs.

Forcing myself to roll over, I used my hands to push up off the ground. Blood trickled down my leg where it had connected with the asphalt, and pain lanced up my leg, radiating throughout my entire being. It felt like fire was burning across my flesh as I hobbled to my feet.

"Take her inside." Javier jerked his head toward the metal building behind me. "I'll be inside in a minute."

Dr. Brooks wrapped his fingers around my bicep and dragged me into the warehouse. It was abandoned, save for a metal cabinet and a few tables and chairs. The smell made my stomach churn with bile, nearly causing me to vomit. I was shoved into a seat with such force, it made me cry out in pain.

"Make one move, and I will kill you." Dr. Brooks hissed through clenched teeth. His voice was laced with venom. "Secure your legs to the chair, and don't fucking try anything," he said, with the weapon trained on my head. "If you so much as kick me, you'll die."

"No." The back of his hand struck my face again.

"Do it." The metal barrel pressed into my scalp.

My eyes closed as I leaned forward and wrapped the plastic around my ankle and pulled it tight. I repeated the process with the opposite leg and sat up.

"There."

"Hold onto the chair arms." He waved the gun at me, waiting for me to comply.

As soon as I did, he tucked the gun into his pants and grabbed more ties. The cold, sharp bite of the zip tie cutting into my wrist sent a jolt of pain up my arm, but it was nothing compared to the terror that gripped my heart. He secured my hands to the arms of the seat with a speed that left me breathless, his movements precise and methodical, as though he had done this a thousand times before. My body was trembling uncontrollably, my skin slick with sweat as the full weight of my predicament settled over me.

"Why are you doing this?" I tilted my eyes toward him.

"Because money talks." He grunted. "Shut up and you'll be fine. Javier plans to use you to get money out of your brothers. He knows who you are, Catarina Anastasi."

"If you know who I am, then you know you won't get a dime from my family. The only thing you'll get is death."

Javier stepped through the door, clapping. "Nice performance. I am not afraid of death, but you should be." He squatted beside me. "Such a shame." His finger trailed down my jaw and along my collarbone. "I could have made you a queen."

"Fuck you." I spit in his face.

Javier laughed as he wiped the spit off his cheek. "Stupid girl." His arm lashed out, his fingers wrapping around my throat. He pulled my body toward him, causing the chair to tilt toward him. The stench of his cigar-stained breath wafted across my skin, his lip mere inches from my own.

"I said I wouldn't hurt you. But you need to be taught a lesson."

Javier slipped a knife from his pocket, the blade glinting beneath the fluorescent lights. I watched as he slipped the blade beneath my scrub top and drew the blade toward my face. The fabric separated with ease, falling open to bare my skin beneath. He pushed the material further apart and cupped my breast.

"I'm going to break you in. A woman like you needs to know your place." Javier used the knife to cut my bra from my body. The cool air caused my nipples to pebble as they were exposed. Tears leaked from my eyes as he ran his hand down the center of my chest. "You will learn your place," he whispered into my ear.

I turned my head away from him, refusing to look at the monster touching me. He continued his exploration of my body, his rough fingers tracing the contours of my exposed breasts.

"Javier," Dr. Brooks said. "This wasn't part of the plan."

"You're not in charge, Gringo. I am. I will do what I please with her, and you will watch, or I will cut off your head." Javier gripped my chin, forcing my eyes to look at him. "When I am done with you, no man will want to touch you."

"Please," I begged, knowing my cries were falling on deaf ears.

His tongue flicked out and traced the line of my jaw to my ear. He pressed his lips close to my head and spoke with such venom, my body shook.

"Maybe I'll just keep you for myself."

I gasped at his words. My body shifted, trying to pull away from his hold, but he tightened his grip. The sensation of something sliding down my hip brought a renewed sense of hope. The tiny screwdriver I'd hidden inside my scrubs was still there. It hadn't fallen out when I was thrown to the ground. Now, if I could only get my hands free, I might be able to save myself from the future hell I was facing.

"I need to make some calls." Javier stepped back, allowing me to breathe. "When I return—" he smirked at me, his eyes filling with lust. "We will become better acquainted. Stanley." He turned to Dr. Brooks. "Have one of the guards help you clear the table off and strap her to it. I'll need it when I come back."

I watched through tear-filled eyes as Javier stalked out of the warehouse, leaving me with Dr. Brooks.

"I didn't take you for a monster." My voice was hoarse from being choked. "Is this what you wanted? To watch that bastard rape me?"

"Shut up," he spat, moving toward the table. "Women throw themselves at him. You should be so lucky he wants you."

"Wants me?" I laughed. "Javier doesn't want me. He only wants to humiliate me. My brothers will kill you when they find me. You think Javier is scary? You should fear La Lama."

"La Lama?" His eyes widened. "He's not real. That's a ghost story told to scare people. And I'm not afraid of your brothers. They don't know Javier and what he is capable of."

"You're a fucking twat," I snorted. "I hope my brother cuts your dick off and shoves it down your throat." For the first time in my life, I was grateful for who I was and where I came from. Being an Anastasi might have come with a burden, but it came with loyalty too. That meant my family was coming for me.

Dr. Brooks cleared the table as Javier ordered, then disappeared out the door, only to return with another man. "Help me get her onto the table."

The guard squatted beside me and used a knife to release the zip ties holding me to the chair. His eyes trailed my body, shimmering with interest when he spied the tattered shirt hanging open.

"I wouldn't touch her. Javier has plans that don't include you marking up her body," Dr. Brooks snapped, causing the man's hand to drop to his side. "Grab her while I cut her hands free, and then we'll carry her over there." He tilted his head toward the table.

He freed my hands, giving me only a moment to react. I tugged out the small screwdriver and jammed it into the guard's neck. Blood spurted out, coating my already ruined scrubs in crimson droplets. His eyes widened in shock as his hand covered the tiny instrument protruding from his throat. I pushed off his stunned frame with my feet, causing the chair to tip backward.

"Motherfucker," Dr. Brooks screamed as he grabbed me by the hair. "You dumb bitch." The blow to my face had me seeing stars as he dragged me across the concrete by the strands he had tangled in his fingers. My hands reached for his hold. The pain was nearly unbearable as he jerked me harder.

His hands scooped me up by my arms and tossed me face first onto the metal table. My stomach connected with the edge, knocking the wind out of my lungs. The hard barrel of a gun pressed into the back of my skull.

"Get on the fucking table, or I'll pull the trigger."

Through swollen eyes, I eased my leg onto the surface and pulled myself up.

"Lie on your back and don't move." I rolled to my side, easing over to my back. "Spread your legs and put your arms over the sides." When I hesitated, his fist connected with my ribs.

Dr. Brooks hovered over me, his eyes glinting with something dark and unsettling. "You brought this on yourself, you know," he murmured, his voice devoid of any real emotion. "If you'd just stayed where you belonged, none of this would have happened."

The words sliced through me, sharp and bitter. A part of me wanted to believe him, to let the guilt swallow me whole. But another part of me, the part that had fought back against every obstacle, every threat in my life, refused to accept that. This wasn't my fault. The blame lay squarely on the shoulders of the men who had taken me, who had seen me as nothing more than a pawn in their game.

As the edges of my vision began to blur again, the cold grip of unconsciousness creeping closer, I made a silent vow to myself—I would survive this. No matter what they did to me, no matter how long it took, I would make it out of this warehouse. And when I did, I would make sure that the men who had put me here would regret ever laying a hand on me.

The world around me faded to black, the last remnants of consciousness slipping away, but that vow burned brightly in my mind, a beacon in the darkness.

nineteen

DONNY

MY BLOOD BOILED with a rage so intense it felt as though my veins were about to burst. An anger that wasn't just a feeling but a living, breathing beast inside me, clawing to get out, ready to burn anyone who dared stand in my way. As we sped toward Reno, all I could think about was how Javier and that damned doctor would regret ever crossing paths with Catarina. They would pay for every second of her suffering, every drop of fear they'd forced into her heart.

"We're meeting Alex at his place. He thinks he has an idea where Javier might be, but he needs to check on some things first." Massimo's voice was steady, but I could hear the underlying tension as he glanced over at me. "We're going to get her back."

"I know." My voice was tight, barely more than a whisper, as I stared out into the inky blackness of the night. Hours had slipped by since Catarina had been taken, and with every passing minute, the scenarios in my head grew darker, more torturous. I couldn't stop imagining what she might be enduring, and each thought twisted the knife deeper into my chest.

Javier was the type of man who took what he wanted without a second thought, without a shred of humanity. And Catarina… she wasn't just beautiful; she was a beacon of light in our world of shadows, a woman who deserved better than this horror. The thought that she might be hurt, violated in ways I couldn't bear to think about, made the blood in my body seethe like molten lava. If I saw her bruised, broken… it would be the end of Javier. I would tear him apart with my bare hands, and the doctor would follow.

Massimo's car was suddenly filled with the sharp ring of his phone. My eyes darted to him as he answered with a swipe on the steering wheel.

"Massimo," Antonio's voice crackled through the car's speakers, tinged with exhaustion. "We've loaded up and are about to head to Vegas. What's your status?"

"We're thirty minutes out." Massimo's gaze flicked to the GPS display, the cold light illuminating his face in the darkness. "Any change in Michael's condition?"

"No," Antonio sighed, the weight of the situation heavy in his voice. "Harley assures me the transport is fine, and his condition is to be expected. I finally got to see all the scans and file on him. We're lucky to have him back in this shape."

"And Harley?" Massimo's voice softened, the concern evident. "Has she settled down about having to go with you?"

"Actually," Antonio paused, as if gathering the strength to continue. "About that. The hospital has informed her that if she leaves them short-staffed, she'll lose her job. And since Catarina's been terminated for not showing up, they expect Harley, as the nursing supervisor, to step up and not take a vacation."

"Tell Harley she'll be hired as Michael's private nurse. I'll make sure she's compensated for this mess."

"I figured as much. Mia's already making space for her at the house."

As Massimo ended the call, my eyes caught sight of Alex standing alone on his stoop, his hands shoved deep into his pockets, his face etched with worry. I couldn't help but wonder what he was thinking, but then again, it didn't matter. I was too far gone, too wrapped up in the tidal wave of fury coursing through me.

"Antonio, we're here. I'll call you when we have Catarina. Make sure the private jet is on standby. I have a feeling we'll need it to bring her home."

"Sure thing. Stay safe, *fratello*."

"He looks pissed," Vincenzo muttered from the back seat, his voice low and dark.

"Yeah, something's up." Massimo parked the car, and we all climbed out, the night air biting against my skin, but I barely felt it.

"What's up?" I asked, my gaze sweeping over the quiet neighborhood. It was too peaceful here, too ordinary. How could the world just go on when Catarina was out there, somewhere, suffering?

"Let's go inside." Alex's voice was strained, and I could see the shadows under his eyes as he led us into his house.

"All right. Spill." Massimo shut the door with a decisive thud, and the room seemed to close in around us.

"I've been suspended," Alex said, his words clipped and bitter. "Accused of being on the take from Javier Costa."

"You've gotta be fucking kidding me." Vincenzo's fists clenched at his sides, his knuckles turning white.

"Nope." Alex ran a hand through his hair, frustration etched into every line of his face. "It doesn't matter, though. I know where Javier is."

"Why didn't you lead with that?" Vincenzo growled. His temper was barely containable.

"Seriously?" Alex snapped, his eyes flashing. "My job is on the line because I didn't follow protocol. I'm going to lose everything I've worked for. And for what? For a mobster. Because that's what you are, right?"

"Yes, that's what we are." Massimo grabbed Alex by the shirt, pulling him close, their faces inches apart. "And right now, my sister is in the hands of a man who's using us as leverage. You can blame us all you want, but my sister—who is the heart and soul of our family—is in the hands of a monster. So, you can either help us, or you can get the hell out of our way."

I closed my eyes, trying to keep the bubbling fury from boiling over. "Are you in or out?" My voice was low, dangerous. "You may hate what we stand for, but you cared for Catarina. Don't forget that."

"Fuck." Alex sighed, his resolve crumbling. "Let me show you what I have."

We spent the next hour pouring over every detail Alex had managed to gather. I could see the conflict in his eyes, the way his morals clashed with his actions. He was a man who had dedicated his life to upholding the law, and now he was breaking it to save a woman he barely knew. But he didn't know us, not really. He didn't understand that beneath the crime, the violence, there was loyalty, there was love. We were a family, and we would tear the world apart to protect our own.

"How far is this warehouse from here?" Vincenzo's voice cut through the tension, his pacing a reflection of the restless energy I felt coiling inside me.

"Twenty minutes." Alex shoved the documents back into a folder, his movements sharp and efficient. "I assume you're armed?" He raised an eyebrow at Massimo.

"Yes."

"Are we going or what?" I couldn't hold back any longer. The words exploded from me, raw and seething. "Catarina is trapped with a monster. God knows what's happening to her. Standing here arguing isn't doing a damn thing to help her."

"Yeah, we're going." Massimo headed for the door, his expression hard. "Alex, thanks for the information."

"Whoa. You aren't going without me." Alex grabbed his jacket, determination replacing the uncertainty in his eyes. "I've gotten this far into the mess. I'm going to see it through."

"This isn't going to end with Javier or the doctor in cuffs. If you think your career is over now, it will be if you get in the car with us."

"I'm coming." Alex pushed past him, climbing into the backseat of Massimo's SUV.

"Looks like we're bringing him home with us, too," Vincenzo muttered as he followed.

As I slid into the front seat, I couldn't help but wonder what the future held. We were gaining allies, but we were also dragging more people into our world, into the darkness that surrounded us. Harley, and now Alex, were becoming part of our family. I knew Harley would fit in; she had the loyalty, the fire.

But Alex? I wasn't so sure.

twenty

CATARINA

EVEN THROUGH THE blurriness of my swollen eyes, I caught a glimpse of Javier as he entered the building. My arms were stretched painfully across the cold metal surface above my head, strapped at an unnatural angle that sent searing jolts of pain down my sides. The edge of the table dug into my back, and my legs were bent and spread open, each ankle bound tight, rendering me completely exposed and vulnerable.

Javier's presence loomed over me, his shadow casting a dark pall across my paralyzed frame. He leaned in close, his breath hot against my skin. My body flinched involuntarily as his fingers began to trace the exposed contours of my flesh, sending shivers of disgust through me. The remnants of my top hung in tatters by my sides, offering no protection. I had once taken pride in my body, in the curves and lines that made me who I was. But now, as his eyes raked over my ample breasts with a sickening gleam of satisfaction, I felt nothing but shame.

"Your skin is beautiful, even covered in ink," he murmured, his fingers following the intricate patterns of my tattoos. Then, without warning, he grabbed one of my breasts, his hand squeezing with cruel force. "But these," he said, a twisted smile curling his lips, "are spectacular."

Hot tears escaped the corners of my eyes, mingling with the blood and bruises that marked my face, streaking down in a silent, salty lament. I could feel the tremors of fear ripple through me as Javier's touch moved to my legs, the anticipation of what was coming suffocating me. I knew what he intended to do. I had seen men like him before—men who used their power to crush women, to remind them of their place. And now, I was just another victim, another trophy to be broken.

The sharp sting of his blade nicking my flesh made me jerk against the restraints. "Be still," he commanded, his voice laced with amusement. "I don't want to cut you—yet." His chuckle was low and menacing as he dragged the blade up the leg of my pants, slicing through the fabric with ease. He repeated the process on the other side, pulling the ruined clothing away with a satisfied grunt. "Beautiful," he whispered, more to himself than to me.

Panic surged through me, and I thrashed against the binds with every ounce of strength I had left. The table beneath me rattled with my efforts, but it was futile. Javier was undeterred, and my struggle only seemed to excite him further. I squeezed my eyes shut, trying to escape into the only refuge I had left—my mind. I forced myself to think of Donny, to think of my family, to think of anything other than the man who was about to violate me. But the moment his fingers invaded me, all illusions shattered. He was inside me, reveling in my humiliation, in the power he wielded over my helpless body.

"Your pussy is going to feel nice, *puta*," he sneered. "Stanley, get over here and watch as I fuck this bitch into submission. When she goes back to her family, I want her broken."

"Javier, is this really necessary?" Stanley's voice was weak, but I could hear the fear in it.

"Yes. Now, get over here, or I'll put a bullet in your head."

I didn't need to look to know that Dr. Brooks—Stanley—had moved to the other side of the table. He might not have been the one torturing me, but his compliance made him just as guilty. I prayed silently that my brothers would make him pay just as dearly as Javier. The moment Javier tore away my underwear, I felt the last shred of protection rip away with it.

Maybe this was my punishment. Maybe God was punishing me for my selfishness, for thinking I could outrun the darkness that came with being an Anastasi. For so long, I had convinced myself that I could lead a normal life, free from the poison of my family's name. But the instant Javier forced himself inside me, I knew how wrong I had been. He wasn't just taking my dignity—he was destroying any chance of happiness I had left, burning it to the ground with each violent thrust.

The metal table beneath me trembled with the force of his assault, and with every shudder, a piece of me shattered. My lip quivered uncontrollably, the tears flowing freely now, pooling beneath me on the cold, unforgiving surface. And then, as suddenly as it began, it was over. Javier pulled away. His breath was heavy as he fixed his zipper. He leaned down close to my ear, his voice dripping with venom.

"Now you know who is in control. And if you get out of here alive, you'll remember that."

twenty-one

DONNY

JAVIER WAS AN AMATEUR. That was the first thing that struck me when we rolled up to the abandoned warehouse. If this had been one of our operations, we'd have had men stationed at every possible entry point, but not here. Just two guys standing guard like they were at some low-level drug drop. And there was Javier, pacing outside on his phone, looking more like a businessman stressed about a deal gone wrong than a man in control of a kidnapping.

"This guy is either really stupid or arrogant," Alex muttered as he cut the engine, the tension in his voice mirroring the knot in my stomach. "The doc must be inside."

"No worries. We've dealt with worse," Massimo said, his voice calm as ever. He stepped out of the SUV, sliding his weapon from the holster at his back. "You coming?"

I joined him at the front of the vehicle, my eyes locked on the men at the entrance. A smirk tugged at my lips as I watched Vincenzo draw his blade from the sheath strapped to his calf. There was a time when he would've resisted that part of himself, the part that

144

knew how to handle the family's darker business. But that was before Riley, before he almost lost everything. Now, he wore that side of himself like a second skin, and in a twisted way, I was glad he had embraced it. We needed that version of Vincenzo tonight.

"One of us needs to check the inside for numbers," Alex said, his sidearm in hand as he moved toward the building. "I'll go."

"Hang on." Vincenzo hurried after him. "I'll go with you."

I watched them disappear around the side of the metal structure, expecting them to get a look inside and come back with a plan. But the next thing I knew, Vincenzo's roar shattered the silence, and I saw him launch himself at one of the guards. My heart leaped into my throat as Alex hollered something at him, but his words were lost in the chaos. He quickly pressed his gun to the head of the other guard, but it was clear we had lost any element of surprise.

"What the fuck, Vin?" Massimo hissed as he kneeled to pull Vincenzo off the man he had just cut down.

Vin's eyes, wild, and dark with rage, met mine. His knife dripped with blood, a stark, crimson contrast against the night. "No more waiting. Catarina needs us now."

Massimo turned toward the building, his expression hardening. "What did you see?"

Vin shook his head, casting a pained glance my way. "Donny shouldn't go in."

His words hit me like a freight train. I pushed past them, rounding the side of the warehouse, my breath coming in ragged gasps. I couldn't wait. I had to see her. But Alex caught my shoulder, his grip firm.

"Donny, wait. You need to prepare yourself. It's bad, and she's gonna need you levelheaded when you get inside. Maybe Vin is right—you should wait until we bring her out."

His plea stopped me in my tracks. The pain in his voice, the fear, it clawed at my insides, making my stomach churn with dread. I shrugged off his hand and pressed myself against the window, my eyes narrowing to peer inside.

What I saw made my world tilt on its axis. Javier and the doctor were arguing about something, but my focus was on the woman lying on the table. Her shirt hung in tatters, her breasts exposed, her legs bound to the table, her pants stripped away. If it hadn't been for the tattoos, I might not have recognized her as Catarina. Her face was swollen, bruised, and bloody, but it was her body—so cruelly exposed, so violated—that broke me. There was no doubt in my mind what they had done to her. I turned my head and vomited into the grass, my entire body shaking with the force of my failure. I had failed her. I had failed to protect the one person who meant every-thing to me.

"Hey." Alex's hand was on my back, steadying me. "Pull yourself together. She needs you to be strong."

I forced myself to look at him, to see the pain in his eyes, the weight of his own guilt. He hadn't known Catarina long, but he was a protector at heart, and right now, he was feeling the same sense of failure that was tearing me apart.

"Where's my brother?" I asked, my voice barely more than a whisper.

"At the entrance," Alex said, nodding toward the front. "Come on. We gotta move fast before Javier comes out and finds his men dead."

"Men?" My mind was still reeling, but I tried to focus.

"Yeah, your friend has some serious rage issues," Alex said with a humorless chuckle that made me pause.

"Fuck," I muttered. That meant Vincenzo had taken down the second guard too. Two bodies bleeding out at the entrance, and we were just getting started. "Let's go."

When we reached the front, the evidence of Vincenzo's fury was clear—two mutilated bodies, dragged off to the side, their blood staining the ground. Massimo's glare met mine, his eyes filled with unspoken questions I wasn't ready to answer. A simple nod from me, and I saw his hands clench into fists, his jaw tightening with rage.

"I'm going to kill this motherfucker," Massimo growled, starting for the door.

"Easy," Alex said, holding him back. "We need to do this smart. As soon as you breach the inner door, everything changes."

"As much as I want to end Javier's life, my focus needs to be on Catarina," I said, my voice trembling despite my efforts to stay calm. "She needs me to be strong. I can fall apart later."

"Let's go." Massimo turned to Alex with a somber tone. "If you go in with us, you'll be ending your career. I understand if you don't want to do this, but if you do…" He paused, choosing his words carefully. "You'll have a place working for me."

Alex nodded, understanding the gravity of the choice before him. He stepped forward, easing the door open, the creak of the hinges sounding like a death knell.

"Doing this the legal way took too long," he said, glancing back at the narrow hallway inside. "There's no question in my mind now."

He stepped inside, determination hardening his features. "Let's end this and get your girl home."

"Massimo, Vin," I paused, my voice thick with emotion. "You need to be ready to see your sister. It's bad, and she's going to be devastated that you two saw her like this. Try to keep it together."

Vin's grunt was filled with frustration, and Massimo gave a grim nod. We were all on the edge, but there was no turning back now.

"Let's go get our girl."

twenty-two

CATARINA

THE NOISE PULLED me out of the fog that had held me captive, dragging me back to a reality I wasn't sure I wanted to face. Shouting echoed in the distance, followed by the sharp cracks of gunfire. My body instinctively flinched against the restraints, causing the plastic straps to bite deeper into my skin. The pain was a cruel reminder that I was still here, still trapped.

"Stop moving," a deep voice commanded, cutting through the haze that clouded my senses. My heart pounded in my chest, my breath hitching in fear. I tried to open my eyes, to see who it was, but they were swollen shut, sealed by the bruises, and swelling that made seeing impossible. Desperation took hold, and I tried to lift my head, but even that small movement felt impossible, like my body was no longer mine to control.

"Please. Let me cut you free," the voice pleaded, softer now, almost gentle.

I felt hands on my ankles, and the pressure that had held me immobile for what felt like an eternity suddenly eased. The bonds loosened, but my limbs were heavy, lifeless, refusing to obey my mind's frantic commands to fight, to flee. I tried to kick out, to protect myself, but the strength I needed was gone, drained away by the terror and the torment I had endured. Fingers brushed my shoulder, and my stomach twisted in fear, expecting the worst.

"Shhh," the voice whispered, warm breath grazing my neck, sending a shiver down my spine. "Catarina. I got you."

The words broke something inside me, and a sob erupted from my lips, raw and uncontrollable. Relief, disbelief, and overwhelming emotion washed over me all at once. They had come for me. My family was here. I wasn't alone anymore.

As the restraints on my wrists were finally released, my arms fell limply to my sides, the sudden rush of blood causing them to tingle painfully. I was free, but I was too weak to move, too exhausted to even keep my head up. Hands were on me, lifting me, cradling me like I was something precious, something worth saving. I let my head rest against the solid warmth of the body holding me, feeling safe for the first time in what felt like forever.

The battle to stay awake was slipping away, the darkness calling me back into its comforting embrace. But just before it claimed me completely, I heard the words that made my heart stutter, a whisper filled with love and pain that wrapped around me like a promise.

"Cuore mio."

And then, there was nothing but the darkness, and the knowledge that I was no longer lost.

twenty-three

DONNY

HER BODY WAS a map of suffering, each bruise and cut telling a story I wished I could erase. The plastic had torn into her flesh, leaving behind angry red lines that marred her once-perfect skin. As I lifted her into my arms, what was left of her top slipped away, and she was utterly exposed, vulnerable in a way that made my heart ache with an unbearable intensity. I felt her trembling against me, her fragile body shaking with pain and fear. The rage that had been simmering inside me flared into a wildfire. I couldn't tear my eyes away from the chaos in the room, but nothing surprised me anymore—not even the sight of Massimo and Javier locked in a brutal fight or Dr. Brooks lying crumpled at Vincenzo's feet.

I ripped off my shirt and wrapped it around her, desperate to shield her from the world that had done this to her. The shirt was a poor substitute for the protection she needed, but it was all I could give her in that moment. My focus shifted as shouting echoed in the room. Javier had Massimo pinned, reaching for a gun that lay just out of reach.

"Massimo!" I cried out, my voice thick with desperation, torn between my best friend and the woman who was my everything.

But fate spared me the decision. I watched, stunned, as Alex pulled the trigger. Javier's body crumpled, and the sound of the gun hitting the floor reverberated through the room like the final note of a tragic symphony. Massimo wiped the blood and brain matter from his face, his expression a mix of shock and disgust.

"Fuck," Massimo muttered, gagging as Alex pulled him to his feet.

"You all right?" Alex asked, his voice steady despite the chaos.

"Yes. I owe you." Massimo glanced down at Javier's lifeless body before turning to look at us. His eyes landed on Catarina, and the concern in them mirrored the torment in my own heart.

"She needs medical attention," I forced out through clenched teeth, barely holding on to my sanity. I knew he could see the same hell I was witnessing—what Catarina had been through was written all over her battered body.

Vincenzo knelt beside us. His voice was gentle but firm. "Let me take her."

"No, Vin. I'm not letting her go. Don't ask me to." My grip on her tightened, as if by holding her closer, I could keep her from slipping away entirely. "Help me up."

Vincenzo supported me as I rose to my feet, Catarina cradled in my arms. He ran a hand over her blood-matted hair and pressed a kiss to her forehead, a tender gesture that nearly broke me. This wasn't how it was supposed to be—she wasn't supposed to be lying here, broken, and bloodied, in my arms.

"We need to cover this up," Alex said, cutting through the tension in the room. "Help me drag the bodies."

Vincenzo followed me outside, his voice low as he spoke into the phone, arranging for the jet that would get Catarina the care she so desperately needed. But I barely registered his words; my entire world had narrowed to the woman in my arms. The one I couldn't afford to lose.

Vin opened the SUV door for me, and I slid inside, still holding Catarina close. The others followed quickly, their movements frantic, but my focus never wavered from her. An explosion rocked the vehicle as the warehouse went up in flames, but it didn't pull my attention from Catarina. Nothing could.

Massimo's eyes scanned her frail body, his expression darkening with every passing second. "Is she breathing?" he asked, his voice thick with worry.

"Yes," I replied, my voice trembling. "Barely."

"What happens now?" Massimo asked, the question hanging heavy in the air. We all knew the answer, but none of us wanted to say it. Catarina's fate was uncertain, and the future seemed bleak.

"Nothing," Alex answered with an eerie calm. "We left it so that all the evidence points to Javier and Dr. Brooks."

Massimo nodded, but his gaze never left Catarina. "She's a fighter. She'll come back from this."

The conviction in his voice was meant to be reassuring, but the tears welling in his eyes told me how much he was struggling to believe his own words. I had been holding it together, but seeing Massimo's raw emotion broke something inside me. A sob burst from my chest, and the tears I had been holding back for so long finally fell. They splashed onto Catarina's pale skin, mingling with the dirt and blood that still clung to her.

"I can't lose her, Vin. She is my everything," I whispered, the words choking me as they left my mouth. "Cuero Mio."

"I know," Vin whispered back, his hand steady on my back, trying to comfort me when nothing could.

The ride to the airstrip was silent except for the low hum of the engine. I kept my eyes on Catarina, willing her to wake up, to give me any sign that she was still there. But she remained motionless, her breathing so shallow it terrified me.

By the time we reached the plane, the others were already in motion, but my world was still reduced to just one person. Harley's sudden appearance was a shock, but I barely registered it, focused entirely on getting Catarina to safety. Harley took over with the efficiency of someone who had seen too much in her life, guiding me as I carried Catarina onto the plane.

The bed was a welcome sight. I laid Catarina down as gently as I could, the bruises on her body stark against the white sheets. Harley was all business, snapping out orders as she prepared to clean and assess the damage. But I couldn't leave her, not now.

"Donny, I need to examine her," Harley said, her voice soft but insistent. "She deserves a little dignity."

The thought of leaving Catarina, even for a moment, was almost unbearable. But Harley was right—Catarina needed privacy, needed whatever small comforts we could give her after everything she'd been through. With a heavy heart, I nodded and stepped out, closing the door behind me.

Massimo was there with clothes, offering me a way to distance myself from the horror of the past hours, if only for a moment. I changed, the motions automatic, my mind already back in that room with Catarina. I sat down beside Vin, exhaustion finally overtaking me. His hand on my leg was the only thing that kept me grounded as the jet lifted off, carrying us away from the nightmare we'd just escaped.

But in the quiet darkness of the plane, the fear remained—what if we hadn't escaped at all? What if Catarina never came back to me? As sleep claimed me, it was her face that filled my dreams, the only light in the darkness that threatened to consume us both.

twenty-four

CATARINA

EVERY NERVE in my body felt like it was ablaze, a relentless, searing pain that contrasted sharply with the soft mattress beneath me. My eyelids were heavy, as if they were glued shut, and every attempt to open them was a struggle against the darkness that threatened to swallow me whole.

"Take it slow," a gentle voice whispered, a hand lightly pressing against my arm, grounding me in the present. "I'm going to wipe your face, okay?"

"Okay." My voice was a raspy croak, the word barely escaping my cracked lips.

A cool cloth brushed against my face, soothing the burning sensation, and making it easier to pry my eyes open. The light hit me like a punch, forcing me to wince and blink rapidly as my eyes adjusted. Harley's familiar face came into view, her expression a mix of relief and concern as she held the cloth in her hand.

"Let me help you sit up." She eased her hand behind my back, slowly lifting me into a sitting position.

"Where…" The word came out rough, scraping against my throat, and I instinctively reached up to touch my neck.

"We're in Vegas. Antonio's place, to be exact," Harley explained, her voice steady as she helped me adjust to the new reality.

"How?" I asked, each word feeling like it was tearing its way out of me.

"That's a long story," she said softly. "But in a nutshell, Donny and your brothers found you. You've been unconscious for three days."

Her words sent a wave of memories crashing into me, the horrifying images of what Javier had done flooding my mind. My body trembled as tears began to fall, the trauma too fresh, too raw to keep at bay.

"Hey… you're safe now," Harley whispered, pulling me into a comforting embrace. But the safety she offered couldn't touch the agony that clawed at my soul.

"He raped me," I breathed, the confession breaking me all over again as it echoed in the room.

"I know, baby," Harley murmured, pressing a tender kiss to my head. "I cleaned you up on the plane. I've given you medication and taken blood to ensure you're clean. Now that you're awake, I want you to take something to prevent pregnancy. Do you think you can swallow a pill?"

The thought of carrying that monster's child sent a fresh wave of panic through me. "I'll make myself do it," I choked out, shuddering at the very idea. Harley handed me a glass of water, and I forced the pill down despite the pain in my throat, the tiny tablet feeling like a jagged stone as I swallowed.

"Where are they?" I asked, my voice shaking as I handed the empty glass back to her.

"Who?"

"Javier and Dr. Brooks." Their names tasted bitter on my tongue.

"They're dead," Harley said with a finality that brought a twisted sense of relief. "I need to let your family know you're awake." She quickly sent a text, then looked at me with a gentle smile. "I'm surprised Donny isn't in here. He hasn't left your side since we arrived."

"I don't want to see him," I blurted out, my heart clenching in fear.

"Catarina, you can't do that. Don't shut him out," Harley urged, her eyes filled with understanding.

"Look at me, Harley. I'm broken. I'm ruined. He deserves someone who hasn't been destroyed," I whispered, the shame and self-loathing curling around my heart like a vice.

"Sweet girl, you aren't destroyed. And that man loves you," she replied, her voice firm, but I could only shake my head, unable to believe her.

"Does he know—"

"That you were raped?" Harley cut me off gently. "Yes. He's the one who cut you from the table, and it was clear to everyone in that room what you'd been through."

"Everyone?" I tensed, horror creeping into my veins. "Who else saw me?"

"It's not important because they don't see you any different," she reassured me, but I needed to know.

"Harley, please," I pleaded, desperate for the truth.

Before she could answer, the door creaked open, and my brother Massimo stepped inside. The sight of him—his face twisted with emotion—made something inside me break. I crumpled into his arms, the sobs ripping from my chest as his own tears mingled with mine.

"I thought we lost you, Cat. I'm so sorry I didn't get to you sooner," he whispered, his voice thick with guilt.

"It's me who should be sorry," I managed through the sobs. "I ran away and walked right into hell. If I hadn't left, none of this would've happened."

"No," he said fiercely, pulling back to look at me. "Don't you dare blame yourself. Javier Costa is the only one to blame. Do you feel up to seeing some visitors?"

"I don't know." I glanced at Harley, who gave me a nod of encouragement.

"Your family needs to see you, baby girl. Mom and Dad are here, as are the twins. You don't have to tell them specifics, but let them see that you're okay," Harley said softly.

"Okay," I agreed reluctantly, my heart racing at the thought of facing them.

The next hour was a blur of tears and embraces. My family's relief was palpable, but the weight of their worry and pain was almost too much to bear. I tried to focus on my sisters. Their comforting presence was a balm to my shattered nerves, but my eyes kept straying to Donny, who stood off to the side, his gaze never leaving me. I couldn't read the emotions swirling in his eyes—fear, sadness, maybe even disgust. I feared he saw me as damaged, as unworthy of his love.

When my family finally left the room, Donny stayed. Harley gave me one last look, brushing a stray lock of hair from my face.

"Remember, he loves you," she whispered before walking past Donny, squeezing his arm in support. He nodded at her, then closed the door, sealing us in the silence that suddenly felt too heavy to bear.

He stood frozen, the turmoil in his expression mirroring the storm inside me. I couldn't stand the tension any longer, so I broke it with the only words I could muster.

"Thank you," I said, my voice cracking as a tear slipped down my cheek.

"For what?" he asked, his voice thick with emotion as he took a tentative step toward me.

"For saving me."

"If I had done my job, you wouldn't need saving," he replied, his voice breaking, the weight of his guilt crushing him.

"Donny," I whispered, reaching out to him. "You can't blame yourself. I ran away. I put myself in danger. This isn't on you." I held my hand out, desperate for the connection only he could give. "Sit with me."

He took my hand, lacing his fingers with mine, and sat on the edge of the bed. His thumb traced over my knuckles, and I could see the tears welling in his eyes, threatening to spill over.

"I nearly lost you, Catarina," he said, his voice trembling with the fear he had been holding in.

"I hate that you saw me like that," I confessed, closing my eyes against the flood of shame. "I can't ask you to stay with me, Donny.

It wouldn't be fair to expect you to deal with the aftermath of what happened."

His eyes snapped to mine, a fierce determination blazing in them. "What are you saying, Cat?"

"I need some time," I said, my voice faltering. "And I'm telling you, it's okay to walk away."

His hand tightened around mine, his grip a lifeline I wasn't sure I deserved. He leaned in closer, his voice low and intense.

"I. Am. Not. Walking. Away," he said, his jaw clenched. "I love you, and not just in good times. I realize you need time to heal, but I'll be beside you while you do. Don't push me away because you're afraid."

"He raped me, Donny," I choked out, the words like poison on my tongue. "I'm tarnished. Broken."

He cupped my chin, forcing me to meet his gaze. "You are not broken. The bruises will heal, as will the internal scars."

"Did you hear what I said? He. Raped. Me," I cried out, the pain of the truth suffocating me.

"It doesn't change how I feel about you. Don't you understand? I love you, goddamn it," he said, his voice fierce with conviction. He leaned in and pressed a tender kiss to my lips, the touch of his mouth on mine more comforting than I could have imagined. "Nothing will change that."

I broke down, burying my face in his chest as the tears flowed freely. "How can you want me after that man ruined me?"

"He didn't ruin you, baby," Donny whispered, gathering me into his arms and sliding behind me on the bed. "It's going to take time, but

I'll be by your side through all of it. Even if it takes years, I'm not going anywhere."

"I don't deserve you," I murmured, the guilt and shame eating away at me.

"I think you have that backward. It's me who doesn't deserve you," he replied, his voice soft but firm.

I leaned into his hold, my eyes closing as exhaustion and pain threatened to pull me under. I didn't know if I could ever give him what he needed, but the selfish part of me couldn't make him go. I might wake up one day to find him gone, but until then, I'd let him carry me through the darkness.

How's Michael?" I asked, my mind drifting to Antonio, and the weight he must be carrying.

"Still not awake," Donny replied, his voice tinged with concern. "Mia's been by his side since they brought him here. Antonio only left to check on you. We're hopeful that being home will help him wake up, but we just don't know. Harley's been incredible, bouncing between you and him, making sure you're both taken care of."

"She's a good woman," I murmured, feeling a pang of guilt for the chaos I'd caused.

"When is she going back?" I asked, trying to focus on something other than the guilt gnawing at my insides.

"She's not," Donny said, surprising me. "The hospital fired her for leaving to help us. But Massimo didn't hesitate—he hired her as Michael's personal nurse."

I felt a fresh wave of guilt crash over me. "I fucked up everyone's life because I didn't want to accept my family. Maybe what happened is my punishment," I whispered, the weight of my decisions pressing down on me like a ton of bricks.

Donny's body stiffened beneath me, his reaction immediate and fierce. "Never say that again, Catarina. What happened to you wasn't punishment. It wasn't your fault. Do you hear me?"

"Yes," I whispered, but the shame lingered, clinging to the corners of my mind.

Donny shifted, gently laying me beside him on the bed. He wrapped his arm around my waist, pulling me close, as if he could protect me from the nightmares that still haunted me. I wanted to find comfort in his embrace, but a part of me was terrified. What if I closed my eyes and woke up back in that warehouse, the horrors waiting for me?

He must have sensed the turmoil churning inside me because he tightened his hold, his voice a soft whisper in the darkness. "You can rest, Cat. I've got you."

TWO MONTHS LATER, I found myself sitting quietly beside Michael's bed, appreciating the rare moment of solitude. Donny had taken Alex to the club to show him a few things, leaving me alone for the first time in days. Antonio and Mia were at a doctor's appointment, grateful that I had offered to sit with Michael. The silence in the room felt heavy but comforting, a quiet that allowed me to gather my thoughts.

"It's strange, you know," I began softly, as if talking to myself more than him. "For weeks, I've been talking to you like we were old friends, spilling my secrets, not knowing I was talking to my brother-in-law the whole time. Secrets," I scoffed, "more like lies I told myself. Running away almost got me killed and ruined the lives of two people. Although, I suspect Harley is happy to be here now."

Harley had been furious when she first arrived in Vegas, but it didn't take long for things to change. Drew was a big part of that. Donny had told me how, the moment Drew laid eyes on her, he knew Drew was in deep. Harley had tried to fight the attraction, but after an afternoon spent fixing a flat tire, the battle was over. We were all pretty sure they had ended up having sex in the back of the

SUV on the side of the road, and now, we suspected they were off eloping.

"I kind of wish you were awake," I sighed, resting my head on the edge of the bed. "I could really use some advice from someone who's not in the middle of this mess. Donny's been amazing, despite how bitchy I've been. I've been seeing a therapist, and she says my moods are normal. She also says my... interest in sex with Donny is normal too. But it doesn't feel normal. I keep thinking I shouldn't want him after everything that happened, but lately, it's all I can think about—him, and, well… his cock." I let out a frustrated breath, feeling the heat of embarrassment creeping up my neck. "But he won't touch me. I'm the one who's embarrassed by how I feel, but deep down, I think he's afraid to admit he's not attracted to me anymore. After all, he saw me strapped to that table, naked and used. I wouldn't want me either."

These were the thoughts my therapist had been helping me work through, trying to show me that what happened to me didn't define who I was. She told me that my desire for intimacy was a sign of healing, but Donny's resistance always sent me spiraling into doubt.

"Maybe I need to admit he doesn't want me like that," I whispered, the words heavy with defeat.

"Or maybe you just need to tell him you want sex," came a rough, familiar voice that made me jerk my head up in shock.

"Michael?" I gasped, standing up so quickly I nearly knocked the chair over. My hands flew to his face, cupping his cheeks as if to confirm he was real. "You're awake. Oh my God."

He blinked at me, his eyes struggling to adjust as he glanced around the room. "Where am I?"

"Do you know who I am?" Panic flared in my chest at the thought that he might not remember. I grabbed the pin light from the drawer and Harley's stethoscope from the bedside table, ready to check him over. He winced as I flashed the light into his pupils, but his reaction was good, even if it made my heart pound.

"Yeah, Catarina, I know who you are," he replied, his voice stronger than I expected. "Are you going to answer me?" His eyes roamed the room, taking in his surroundings, then his expression darkened. "He cut off my fingers."

"Michael," I said, trying to keep my voice steady, "You've been in a coma for months. We didn't think you would survive, but you did. You're home, and you're safe."

His gaze sharpened. "Dmitri?" he asked, his voice low, filled with a mixture of fear and hatred.

"Dead," I answered simply, grabbing my phone, and quickly pressing the speaker button. "Hey, Catarina. We're headed back now," Antonio's voice came through the line.

"He's awake," I blurted out, barely able to contain the rush of emotions.

"What did you say?" Antonio's voice was thick with disbelief.

"She said I'm awake," Michael answered, leaning across the bed to speak into the phone.

"Michael." Antonio's voice cracked with emotion. "We'll be there in ten."

Michael frowned as the line went dead. "He hung up."

"He's probably in shock," I said gently. "And he needs to focus on driving. The last thing he needs is to wreck with Mia in the car."

Michael's frown deepened. "What's wrong with Mia?"

I smiled, a little secret thrill running through me. "Nothing's wrong with her, but you have a surprise coming. I'm going to let them give it to you."

"Shit," Michael muttered, sitting up and adjusting himself against the pillows. "Back to you," he said, turning his attention back to me. "You need to tell Donny how you feel. If I had to guess, he's afraid to take it to the next level."

"Wait. You could hear me?" I asked, stunned.

"Your voice is all I've heard… well, until recently," he admitted, rubbing a hand down his face. The months in a coma had taken their toll on him. He looked thinner, his once muscular frame now much leaner, but he was still Michael, and for that, I was grateful.

The sound of a door slamming downstairs made both of us look toward the hallway. Moments later, the door burst open, and Antonio rushed in, his eyes red-rimmed, his face wet with tears.

"Michael," he whispered, crossing the room in two strides, and pulling his brother into his arms. Both men crumbled together, their sobs filling the room with a heartbreaking echo of relief and sorrow.

I watched them, feeling like an outsider intruding on an intensely personal moment. They kissed and hugged. The love between them was palpable and overwhelming.

"Antonio," I said softly, not wanting to interrupt but knowing I had to. "Mia is waiting." I nodded toward the hallway where Mia stood, tears streaming down her face as she watched the reunion.

"Tell her to come in," Michael said, his voice shaky but steady.

"There's something you need to know first," Antonio said, taking a step back but keeping his hands on Michael's shoulders. "Not too long after you went missing, we got some news that kept us going, even when we thought we'd lost you. Mia," he called out, beckoning her into the room, "Mia found out she was pregnant. With your baby."

Michael's eyes widened in shock as Mia crossed the room to stand beside him. His hand trembled as he reached out to touch the swollen curve of her belly, his face a mixture of awe and disbelief.

"You're having my baby?" he whispered, tears welling up in his eyes as he looked between Mia and Antonio.

The tenderness of the moment was too intimate, too personal, for me to witness. Smiling, I slowly eased out of the room, closing the door softly behind me. As I turned, I collided with a solid wall of muscle.

"Shit," I muttered, startled to find myself face-to-face with Donny.

"Antonio called Massimo… who called everyone. How is he?" Donny asked, his voice full of concern.

I smiled up at him, the relief I felt shining through. "He's weak but awake. He remembers everything, which is a good sign. I felt like they needed some time alone."

Donny nodded in understanding, but his eyes remained on me, filled with a mix of emotions. "How are you?"

I tilted my head, studying him, feeling the weight of everything I had kept inside pressing down on me. "Good. Actually—" I took a deep breath. "Can we talk for a minute?" I watched as his posture stiffened at my request, tension radiating from him. "Please? I have some things I need to say."

"Sure," he said, his voice tight. "Let's go into Harley's room. She and Drew won't be back for a while."

I followed him down the hall, my heart pounding as we stepped into Harley's room. The space was quiet, filled with the scent of her perfume and the faintest hint of Drew's cologne. The bed was neatly made, and I suddenly felt a wave of nerves. This conversation was long overdue, and I wasn't sure how it would end.

twenty-six

DONNY

CATARINA CLOSED the door behind her and took a deep, steadying breath. I'd been waiting for this moment, dreading, and hoping for it all at once, ever since I noticed her pulling away. She'd been hiding behind a wall of pain and fear, and though I caught glimpses of the woman I fell in love with, that wall felt as impenetrable as Mount Rushmore. I was bracing myself for another conversation where she'd push me away, but instead, she shocked me.

"I'm ready to take this to the next level," she said, her voice steady but her eyes betraying a flicker of vulnerability.

"Catarina, I—" My head snapped up to meet her gaze.

"What did you just say?"

"I said—" she took a step closer to me, her eyes locked on mine. "I'm ready to take our relationship to the next level."

I blinked, completely thrown off balance. "I don't understand." I shook my head, trying to process her words. This wasn't what I was expecting her to say.

"My therapist… she's been helping me see things differently," Catarina began, her voice trembling slightly. "She said I need to stop using what happened to me as an excuse to push away the people who love me. I told her I was scared of what you'd think if you knew I wanted to be with you intimately, and that's why I've been distancing myself."

I felt a jolt of pain at her words, the idea that she believed I could ever be anything but understanding. "You thought I'd be what? Disgusted that you wanted me?" I asked, my voice barely above a whisper, stunned by her admission.

"Yes," she confessed, her eyes shining with unshed tears. "I was raped, Donny. Most women… they can't bear the thought of intimacy after something like that. But my therapist keeps telling me that the rape is something that happened to me, not something that defines me. It's not who I am." She blew out a frustrated breath, clearly struggling with the weight of her emotions.

"Catarina," I murmured, stepping closer to her, closing the space between us. I pressed her gently against the door, needing her to feel the sincerity in my words. "I've never stopped wanting you. Your therapist is right—what happened to you is just that, something that happened. It doesn't define you, and it damn sure didn't change anything about the way I feel about you."

She gasped as I pressed my hips into her, letting her feel exactly how much I still desired her. I wanted her to understand just how deeply my feelings ran, that nothing—not even the hell she'd been through—could change that.

"I've kept my distance because I wanted you to be ready, Catarina," I continued, my voice thick with emotion. "I told you I would wait an eternity for you to be ready—I meant it."

Her breath hitched, and I could see the uncertainty warring with the desire in her eyes. She reached out, her hand trembling slightly as she ran it down my cheek, her touch sending a shiver of electricity through me. "I'm ready," she whispered, her voice filled with a quiet determination that made my heart ache. "I need to know that part of me isn't broken, Donny. And you're the only man I want to show me I'm still whole."

The raw honesty in her words shook me to my core. She stood on her toes and pressed her lips to mine. At first, her touch was tentative, soft, but then something shifted, and her hands found their way into my hair, tugging with a desperation that mirrored my own.

I was barely holding on by a thread, my self-control fraying as every part of me wanted to give in to her, to lose myself in the connection we had. But I knew I had to be careful. She'd been through so much, and the last thing I wanted was to push her too fast.

"Baby," I murmured against her lips, pulling back slightly to meet her eyes. "I appreciate that you say you're ready, but don't you think we should take it slow?"

Her eyes searched mine, the vulnerability in them making my heart twist. "Donny, I know you're trying to protect me, but I don't want to go slow," she said, her voice firm but laced with an edge of uncertainty. "I need this…I need you. I want to feel something other than fear and pain. I want to feel alive again, and I want that with you."

Hearing her say that, knowing what it took for her to get to this point, nearly undid me. I cupped her face in my hands, my thumbs brushing away the tear that slipped down her cheek. "Catarina, I want you to feel safe with me, more than anything. I'll give you whatever you need, whatever you want, but I need you to promise me one thing."

"What's that?" she whispered, her eyes wide, searching mine for answers.

"Promise me that you'll tell me if it's too much if you need to stop. I don't want to hurt you, Cat. I could never live with myself if I did."

"I promise, now…fuck slow." Catarina slid her hand between our bodies and cupped the bulge pressing against the zipper of my pants. "I need fast and hard, Donny. I don't need to stop and think because that's when the memories sneak in." She flicked the button on my pants and slipped her hand inside.

"Christ." I gritted my teeth as her fingers wrapped around my shaft. "Catarina. We're in your friend's room."

"I. Don't. Care." She stroked me beneath my jeans.

The strength I had trying to remain gentlemanly cracked into a thousand pieces. I tugged her hand out and lifted her into my arms. Her legs wrapped around my back as I spun us toward the bed.

"You're going to owe your friend new linens." I laid her down and shoved her shirt up. "Because I'm going to remind you who you are. You're not what happened to you, Catarina. You're the woman I love." I pressed my lips to her belly. "You're the woman I can't live without." I tugged her bra down, exposing her nipple. My fingers pinched the pink bud, making her body arch into mine. "You're the woman I'm going to marry."

Catarina gasped as I tugged her pants down and tossed them to the floor.

"If you're having second thoughts, tell me now. We can stop."

"Don't stop," she moaned, wiggling her hips against me.

"Look at me," I demanded, her eyes on mine. "You're in control. If you say no, this stops immediately, okay?"

She nodded.

"I need to hear you say it, Catarina—or it ends now."

"I understand."

Seeing the truth in her eyes, I dipped my face between her thighs and flicked my tongue across her sweet folds. Catarina tensed, but not in a way that made me pause. Her body was screaming for more, so I gave it to her. Thoughts of what happened were driven out of my head by the sounds coming from her. She was desperate for a new memory—almost manic.

"Catarina," I mumbled against the soft flesh. "I want to touch you here." I slid my finger through her slit.

She didn't need to say a word; the subtle widening of her legs spoke volumes, telling me she was ready, that she trusted me with this moment. Holding her gaze, I gently pushed a finger inside her, pausing to let her adjust, to make sure she was okay. Her inner walls fluttered around me, drawing me deeper into her warmth, and I felt her body responding to every movement. Catarina's eyes fluttered closed as a soft moan escaped her lips, the sound filling the room and sending a jolt of desire straight through me.

She was a vision of pure, unfiltered need. Her skin had taken on a rosy hue, flushed with the intensity of her desire, and her face was relaxed, completely open, trusting me to guide her through this. I moved my hand slowly, letting her feel every inch of the connection between us as I began to pump my fingers in a steady rhythm. My eyes never left her face, watching every flicker of emotion, every slight change as I added another finger, increasing the pressure, the depth.

Her body responded instantly, her back arching slightly as her breathing quickened. The trust in her expression, the way she was surrendering herself to me, made my chest tighten with an overwhelming mix of love and desire. I needed more—I needed to taste her, to feel her unravel beneath my touch.

I leaned down, pressing the tip of my tongue against her swollen nub, giving it a gentle flick. That was all it took for her to let go completely. Her core tightened around my fingers, her muscles contracting as the wave of her orgasm crashed over her. She moaned louder, her hands clutching at the sheets, her body trembling with the intensity of it all.

I could feel the rush of her release, her essence flooding my palm, coating my fingers with the sweetness of her desire. I didn't stop, drawing out her pleasure, savoring every second as she rode the wave, her body trembling, her breaths coming in soft, rapid pants.

She tugged my body up and I covered her lips with my own. "Condom," she whispered against my lips as I plundered her mouth.

"No. You're mine, Catarina. There will never be any barriers between us."

She stiffened beneath me. "Donny. I can't put you at risk." Her eyes glistened with emotion.

Needing her to understand nothing mattered to me but her, I pushed inside her. She arched against me, her throaty moan telling me she was fine. "We are in this together, *cuore mio*. Your struggles are my struggles." I flexed my hips, driving my cock deeper. "I will never need protecting from you." I fastened my mouth over hers as my fingers laced with hers.

Catarina wrapped her legs around me, her heels pressing into my ass.

"Please," she murmured against my lips, "I need…" She arched into me as my shaft brushed against the spot that would send her flying.

"Please what?" I eased out, watching as my dick slipped between her folds.

"Harder." She tugged me back inside with her feet.

"Watch, Catarina. I want you to see me owning your pussy."

Catarina glanced between us, her eyes hooded with desire as she watched my cock ease out and slam back in. Releasing her hands, I shifted so I was leaning back on my heels. I lifted her body, angling her so I could drive myself deeper into her. I pressed my palm over her clit and rubbed.

"Oh my God." She fisted the sheets as I pistoned into her. "I'm gonna—" A scream tore from her lips. Her body contorted beneath me as she tensed and cried out. My own orgasm ripped out of me as her walls clamped down around my steel rod and milked my cum into her core.

"Fuck," I cried out as beads of sweat rolled down my face. "Catarina." I said her name through the sparks and flames of our union. Needing to feel her, I tugged her into my lap and kissed her with every ounce of passion I had. The ripples of her orgasm continued to beat around my shaft even as I held her.

Catarina's head fell against my shoulder, and I felt the warmth of her tears as they trickled down my back. Her body began to shake, and my heart clenched with panic. The telltale signs of her crying sent a wave of fear rushing through me.

"Did I hurt you?" My voice trembled with concern as I instinctively rubbed her back, trying to comfort her. "Catarina? Answer me. Did I hurt you?"

She lifted her head, her eyes locking onto mine, and I saw something in her gaze that took my breath away. "No," she whispered, her voice thick with emotion. "You healed me." And then her lips were on mine, soft and tender, filled with a depth of feeling that made my chest ache.

I pulled back, cupping her face in my hands as I stared into her eyes. The words tumbled out of me before I could stop them. "Marry me."

"What?" Catarina blinked, her tears still glistening on her cheeks.

"Marry me," I repeated, my voice firmer, more certain. "Let me love you for an eternity and then some. Let me give you my last name and make you mine forever. I've loved you since we were kids, Catarina. I am nothing without you, and I don't want to go another day without you sharing my last name. Say yes, and I promise you a life filled with love and devotion. *Cuore mio...* you're my heart. It will never beat for another."

A single tear rolled down her cheek, splashing onto my chest. I held my breath, praying I hadn't spoken too soon, that she was ready to hear what I wanted more than anything. She didn't pull away; instead, she tightened her arms around my neck, her eyes never leaving mine.

"I love you, Donny," she whispered, her voice steady despite the tears. "I ran from you once, and it was the biggest mistake I ever made. It nearly took me from you, but it's always been you for me, too. You say I'm your heart? Well, you're mine. You've stood by me, loved me even when I was broken. How could I ever walk away from a man like that?" She pressed her lips to mine, sealing the promise with a kiss. "Yes... a million times, yes." Her body responded to me, her core pulsing around me as she whispered, "Make me a Russo. Make me your wife."

With those words, every doubt, every fear melted away. We spent the next hour wrapped up in each other, exploring the connection that had always been there but had only grown stronger with time. I gave her all of me, and she gave herself to me completely. In that moment, I knew that nothing would ever take this woman from me again. She was burned into my soul, her life entwined with mine in ways that defied explanation. Together, we could overcome anything.

As we dressed, Catarina's smile was radiant, lighting up the room. "I love you, Donny."

"I love you, *cuore mio*," I replied, pulling her close. "Let's go see about your family. I'm sure they're wondering what we've been doing in here."

She chuckled softly as we walked toward the door. "I doubt that. I wasn't exactly quiet." Her laughter was infectious, and I couldn't help but smile at her honesty. "They're going to be happy about this. They already love you like family, and now it just guarantees I won't be running away again."

"I'd follow you anywhere," I said, my voice filled with conviction. "You're never getting away from me again, Catarina."

"I know," she whispered, resting her head on my shoulder as we stepped out into the hallway. "This is where I belong."

And as we walked together, side by side, I knew that nothing had ever felt more right. This was the beginning of our forever, and I was ready to face whatever came our way, as long as she was by my side.

twenty-seven

DONNY

SIX MONTHS HAD PASSED, but it felt like a lifetime since everything had changed. I stood there, watching my brother Antonio as he clasped hands with Mia and Michael. The ceremony was simple but powerful, a quiet testament to the bond they had forged together. Michael had started to fill out, his frame slowly regaining the strength it had lost. It was almost like seeing him as the man he had been before—before all the pain, before the coma that had stolen so many months from us all. Yet, I could still see the shadows of those lost months in his eyes, a reminder of how fragile our lives had become.

Massimo and Vincenzo stood off to the side, grinning at our younger sibling as the binding ceremony came to its conclusion. Mia was positively glowing, and I couldn't help but marvel at how radiant she looked, especially so soon after giving birth. I suspected her glow came from more than just motherhood; it was the glow of a woman who was deeply, utterly in love. And not just with one man, but with both.

Madison stood close by, cradling their tiny son in her arms. Her eyes sparkled with a longing I knew all too well. She had watched as one by one, the people she loved had found their happiness, their forever. Everyone had managed to get married before her and Massimo, even though they'd been engaged the longest. I'd once asked her how she felt about that, expecting some bitterness, some sadness, but she had only smiled—a wistful, knowing smile—and said their time would come. She wasn't about to rush off to some Vegas chapel just to make it happen. She was content to wait, to let their love blossom in its own time.

Massimo's gaze rested on Madison, curiosity mingling with something deeper, something more profound. When he noticed me watching him, he smiled, a small, private smile that made me suspect their wait wouldn't last much longer. They were just waiting for the right moment, the moment when everything would align perfectly for them. I found myself mildly surprised they hadn't already started their family—after all, it seemed like the thing to do in our family. Babies were becoming the new normal. A soft grin tugged at my lips as my hand drifted to my flat stomach.

Donny was beside me, his presence warm and reassuring as always. He leaned in closer, his arm draped possessively across the back of my chair. "Are you okay?" His voice was gentle, laced with concern. He had a way of knowing when something was off with me, even when I tried to hide it.

I nodded, offering a small smile. "I'm fine."

"Catarina," he whispered, his voice barely audible. "You can tell me anything. I know something's wrong. You haven't been yourself lately."

A sigh escaped me as I rested my head against his shoulder, letting his warmth envelop me. "I've just been tired, that's all."

"Maybe you're pushing yourself too hard. You didn't have to go back to work so soon."

His words were tender, but I could hear the undercurrent of worry that had been a point of tension between us. After Michael had finally woken up, Harley and I had jumped at the chance to return to the ER, eager to reclaim some sense of normalcy. My old boss had been thrilled to have me back, and Harley was a natural fit. But Donny had been resistant, scared that being back in that environment would dredge up memories best left buried. But it hadn't, and I was okay—more than okay. Work had been a balm for my soul, a way to reconnect with the person I'd been before everything fell apart.

"Donny, we've talked about this. I love my work, and it's been good for me," I said softly, watching as Celestina and Alex engaged in a heated conversation. Alex had struggled when he first arrived in Vegas, the city of sin not being kind to a man like him. But after losing his badge and narrowly avoiding jail time on a false accusation, he'd given in to Massimo's offer to work for him. Now, he was head of security at Vekvet Ace Lounge and Casino, and it seemed to suit him.

"I know." Donny's lips brushed my forehead, the warmth of his kiss seeping into my skin. "I just can't help worrying about you. I love you too much not to."

"And I love you," I replied, sitting up and placing my hand on his knee. "But you've got to lighten up. Besides," I paused, my smile growing, "I'll be taking a leave of absence in six months, anyway."

"A leave of absence?" Donny's fingers played with the gold band on my left hand, the one we'd exchanged in a quiet, private ceremony much to my parents' dismay. We hadn't wanted the big wedding, the pomp and circumstance. We'd just wanted each other.

"Yes."

He narrowed his eyes at me, suspicion creeping into his expression. "Catarina, what aren't you telling me?"

Before I could respond, the sound of clapping drew our attention back to the front. Antonio, Michael, and Mia were walking down the center aisle, Madison handing off their newborn son to Mia with a kiss. I was on my feet before I realized it, stepping into their path with a wide smile.

"Congratulations, baby brother," I said, pulling Antonio into a tight embrace. "I'm so happy for you all."

Michael was next, wrapping his arms around me in a hug that felt like coming home. "Have you told him?" he whispered into my ear, his voice low and full of meaning.

I shook my head, feeling the weight of the secret I'd been carrying for weeks. Michael and I shared something special, a bond that no one else questioned. During his coma, I had talked to him every day, my voice a lifeline for both of us. He'd later confided in Antonio that he remembered everything, every word I'd spoken to him during those dark days. It had forged a connection between us, one that made him the person I turned to when I needed to unburden myself. He knew things about me that not even Harley did.

"Don't make him wait," Michael said, pressing a kiss to the top of my head before stepping back to join Mia and their son. "Waiting is torture for those who love you."

Donny's eyes flickered with suspicion as he watched us. "What's he talking about?" he asked, his voice tinged with frustration.

"I love you," I said, leaning in to press a soft kiss to his lips.

"Catarina, stop avoiding my questions. Please." His voice was desperate now, his eyes pleading with me to let him in.

Antonio chuckled as he and the others headed off toward their house. "We'll see you two at the house."

As they walked away, I turned back to Donny, who was still watching me intently. I reached out, brushing my fingers down his face, tracing the familiar lines that I knew so well. "Donny," I whispered, feeling the weight of the moment settle between us. "When I said nothing was wrong, I meant it. But there is something… something that's going to change everything."

"Change everything?" He shook his head, confusion knitting his brows together.

"Yes." I laced my fingers with his, pulling his hand toward my belly and placing it gently against the barely-there bump. "This."

Donny's gaze followed our joined hands, his eyes widening as realization dawned on him. His expression shifted from confusion to shock, and then to something so pure, so full of love, that it took my breath away. A lone tear slipped down his cheek, falling onto our hands as he looked up at me, his eyes full of questions.

I nodded, my own eyes welling up with tears. Words weren't necessary in that moment, not when the truth was laid bare between us.

"You're—" His voice broke, and he hastily wiped at the tears gathering in his eyes. "We're having a baby?"

"Yes," I whispered, my heart swelling with love for this man who had given me everything I never knew I needed.

Donny's hand slipped behind my neck, pulling me into a kiss that was both tender and fierce. His lips moved against mine, his other hand still pressed against my abdomen, holding onto the new life we had created together. When he finally pulled back, he rested his forehead against mine, his breath mingling with mine in the quiet evening air.

"You've given me more than I could have ever asked for," he murmured, his voice thick with emotion.

"It's you who's given me the world, Donny. You brought me back to life after everything that happened in Lake District and Reno. I thought I'd never be whole again, but you breathed life back into me with your love. And now…" I placed our hands more firmly against my belly, feeling the flutter of new life beneath my skin. "Now we're going to have a baby."

Donny pulled me into his arms, holding me close as if he could protect us both from the world. We stood there for what felt like forever, wrapped in each other's warmth, in the promise of what was to come. This was the life I had tried to run from, the life I had been so desperate to escape. But being held by Donny, I realized that I didn't need to run from who I was. I just needed to embrace it, to embrace the love that had found me, and to let it shape the future we were building together.

"I love you, *cuore mio*," Donny whispered, pressing his lips to my forehead.

I pressed closer to him, breathing in his familiar scent, the scent that grounded me, that reminded me of everything we had been through and everything we had yet to face. He was my air, my soul, my everything. And in that moment, I whispered the truth I had been holding onto for so long.

"Your heart forever."

CELESTINA

MY HEAD FELT like it was splitting open, as if a thousand wild horses were stampeding through my skull. I groaned, blinking against the pain as I tried to make sense of where I was. Everything was a blur, my thoughts foggy and disjointed. It took me a few seconds to realize I was inside a moving truck—a truck I had no memory of getting into. Panic surged through me like ice water in my veins.

Where am I? What happened?

I shot upright, adrenaline forcing me into action. My arm flung out instinctively, catching the driver across the face. The seatbelt jerked me back against the seat, locking me in place, but not before the truck swerved violently across the interstate. The driver, Chris—or at least I thought that was his name—gritted his teeth and yanked the steering wheel, fighting to regain control of the vehicle.

My breathing quickened, each breath feeling too shallow, too rapid. I could feel myself teetering on the edge of hyperventilation as the realization hit me like a ton of bricks—I had been kidnapped.

Desperation clawed at my chest, and I fumbled with the seatbelt, trying to free myself, trying to escape.

"Sit still, or you're going to fucking get us killed!" His voice was a low growl, filled with frustration and something darker that made my blood run cold. Before I could react, his hand lashed out, connecting with my face. The force of the slap was enough to stun me, the sting spreading like wildfire across my cheek. For a split second, I was paralyzed by shock, my mind struggling to catch up with what had just happened.

"Fuck," he muttered under his breath, wrestling the truck onto the shoulder of the road. The moment he slammed on the brakes, I seized my chance. My fingers found the door handle, and I yanked it open with every ounce of strength I could muster, flinging the door wide before the truck even came to a full stop.

My legs wobbled as I hit the pavement, betraying me at the worst possible moment. I felt like a newborn calf, unsteady and weak, my limbs unable to support me. I crashed to the ground, the pain radiating through my body as I tumbled down a short embankment. The world spun around me as I rolled, coming to a stop only when I collided with a line of barbed wire that tore into my skin. The pain was sharp and immediate, a cruel reminder that this nightmare was far from over.

My dress—or what was left of it—snagged on the twisted metal, but I couldn't afford to stop. I ripped the fabric free, gritting my teeth against the pain, and tried to push myself up. But my arms were weak, trembling from the effort, and my body felt impossibly heavy. Mud clung to me, seeping into my mouth, the bitter taste mingling with the metallic tang of blood.

Footsteps. Heavy, relentless, getting closer.

Panic surged anew, and I turned to see him—Chris—sliding down the embankment after me, his eyes locked onto mine with a terrifying determination. Fear gave me the strength to move, just a few inches, but it wasn't enough. My fingers dug into the wet grass, pulling me forward, inch by agonizing inch. I spat out the mud that coated my lips, my breath coming in ragged gasps.

Tears blurred my vision, stinging my eyes as I fought against the inevitable. I could feel his presence looming over me, his shadow stretching across the ground as he closed the distance between us with terrifying ease. I kicked out at him, a last-ditch effort fueled by sheer terror, but it was pathetic, a mere swipe that did nothing to deter him.

"Get away from me!" My voice cracked, hoarse and desperate, the sound of it almost unrecognizable to my own ears. But my feeble attempt only gave him the leverage he needed. His hand clamped around my ankle, yanking me back toward him with frightening strength.

"No. Noooooo!" My scream ripped through the air, but it was cut short as his hand closed around my throat, squeezing just enough to silence me without cutting off my air entirely.

"Stop, Celestina," he commanded, his voice cold and devoid of any emotion. The sound of my name on his lips sent a shiver of dread through me, the final nail in the coffin of my hope.

His grip tightened, and I could feel the strength draining from my body, my vision beginning to blur at the edges. My fingers clawed at his hand, but it was like trying to fight against iron. Every instinct in me screamed to keep fighting, to not give up, but my body was betraying me, growing weaker with each passing second.

Please, no, this can't be happening...

But the darkness was creeping in, and I was powerless to stop it. My thoughts became disjointed, fragmented. The last thing I saw was his face, impassive and terrifying, as the world around me faded to black.

What happens when the Reaper falls for an angel?

In a world where love is a liability and monsters lurk in every shadow, he'll risk it all to protect the one thing he was never meant to have—her.

Find out in the next installment: Savage Hearts

playlist

War-Torn Lovers *(Ed Breedlove)*

Hate to Love You *(Karmin)*

Bad At Love *(Halsey)*

Now Or Never *(Halsey)*

Broken Glass *(Mia Platten)*

End Game *(Taylor Swift, Ed Sheeran)*

Fuck Apologies *(JoJo, Whiz Khalifa)*

Meant To Be *(Bebe Rexa)*

Only Want You *(Skylar Simone)*

STFU & Hold Me *(Liz Huett)*

Quit You *(Lost Knights)*

Don't Say Goodbye *(Aaron Carter)*

Tell Me You Love Me *(Demi Lovato)*

Love So Soft *(Kellly Clarkston)*

Deadly Intentions Playlist on Spotify

about dori

"Love, Loyalty, and the Occasional Gunshot."

Dori Pulitano, a USA Today Bestselling Author, is the naughtier, much dirtier half Author LC Taylor. Writing men in shades of grey, the bad girl Dori embraces her Italian side with heroic hitmen, decadent conflicted dons, and oh-so-f*ckable assassins trying to trade their devilish ways for salvation—and the perfect woman to tie to their bed.

And F**k following the rules... this author is most definitely trigger-happy.

visit www.AuthorDoriPulitano.com to learn more.

facebook.com/AlphaBookBoyfriend

instagram.com/alphabookboyfriends

tiktok.com/@alphabookboyfriend

bookbub.com/authors/dori-pulitano

www.ingramcontent.com/pod-product-compliance
Lightning Source LLC
Chambersburg PA
CBHW060319310726
48976CB00007B/2381